I REMEMBER EVERYTHING

A DARK AND TWISTY PSYCHOLOGICAL THRILLER

MARNIE VINGE

YELLOW TRUCK MEDIA, LLC

Editor: Collette Carmon

Ebook ISBN: 979-8-9880918-6-8

Paperback ISBN: 979-8-9880918-9-9

www.marniewritesthrillers.com

For all of y'all who watched Anaconda with Jennifer Lopez too much as a kid, just like me.

ONE

THIS TRIP to the Amazon was my idea. Shoving me overboard from the second deck of the riverboat was my husband's.

As someone forces me upright, soaked and bleeding on the deck, I hack water from my lungs with a throbbing at the back of my skull. I remember only those two hot palms against my bare back and the jarring impact of my head against the edge of the boat.

The wound throbs, and I feel a wetness gathering at the base of my skull that has nothing to do with river water. Blood, warm and thicker than the river. I reach back, touching my scalp gingerly, and draw my hand into my field of vision. The amount of blood shocks me, tunneling my vision and making me nauseated. I roll to the side and vomit onto the deck.

"Breathe, Steph." My name sounds strange, like it's coming to me through a tunnel. Waterlogged ears make it hard to hear clearly, but I recognize the voice.

Steve. My husband.

My eyes shoot open and I look at him, unsure what I'm going to find on his face, knowing that he pushed me. But he looks down at me with concern, sheer terror in his eyes at the prospect of losing me. An interesting dichotomy of emotions since he just tried to end my life.

I recoil from him, scooting backward against the uniformed deckhand holding me upright. It's a feeble attempt at putting distance between us, and Steve kneels at my side, taking my hand. Fighting the urge to pull back and reach for the perfect stranger holding me up, I let Steve have it and look into his eyes, searching them for meaning.

But when Steve looks at me, relief floods his face and his concerned mouth breaks into a smile. A smile I'd know anywhere. The same smile he gave me at the altar on our wedding day. The thought is chilling.

I stare back, unblinking, my face expressionless, hoping that he can't discern the terror I feel.

Is he just going to pretend like everything's fine?

It's an idea so suffocating that I gasp for air.

"Breathe," he repeats, squeezing my hand.

I shake out a nod that seems to go on endlessly, my head waggling before him, desperately trying to show that I'd never consider anything else.

"We need to take her to the infirmary," a woman's voice rises above the chaos.

With a slight French accent, she takes command of the scene and two deckhands show up with a narrow stretcher with the boat's name embroidered on it. *Jaguar.*

The tagline from their brochures hangs below in finer print. *The trip of a lifetime.*

Indeed.

They shuffle me onto the stretcher and carry me down the hallway, Steve following behind. We go below deck and arrive in a tiny white room with a small cot on one wall. Beside it is a stool and a small set of cabinets with a desk below. Thank God I'm not in need of emergency surgery. Or at least I don't think I am.

Internal injuries could make me hemorrhage rapidly. I try not to think about it as they deposit me onto the bed. Steve rounds the corner into the room, his hand lingering on the doorframe and his shirt partially unbuttoned and hanging loosely against his chest. When he approaches, I notice the top button is missing.

"Mrs. Silkwood," the French woman's voice breaks my train of thought. She enters the tiny room and claims the stool next to the cot, forcing Steve to take a step back. I'm grateful for that, but I want a moment alone with her. I want to tell her what happened, but he seems hellbent on staying by my side. If the tables were turned, I'd do what he's doing now. "Roll over onto your side for me."

I do as she says, following her gesture to turn myself to face the wall. She snaps on a pair of gloves and examines my scalp. Cringing at the first touch, I contort my face with pain as she looks it over.

"You'll need stitches," she says.

I say nothing, unable to find my voice at that moment.

"Is that alright?" she asks me.

When I don't answer, she turns around, her voice

more distant, and repeats the question for Steve to answer. I assume he nods because he says nothing, but the woman returns to her work at my scalp.

"I won't be able to numb you, so you'll feel some pressure and possibly a little pain," she says.

My body tightens, each muscle tensing in anticipation of the suture needle's first prick. I think about the moment right before I went over the railing into the water. Inhaling, I feel the spot below my rib cage that's sore from the impact against the balcony. Concrete proof that I went over the railing of the boat from the second story, as if the bleeding at my skull isn't enough.

I wonder if she can see the palm prints on my skin. If Steve's large hands bruised me. Did he push me hard enough for that to happen?

I search my mind for the moments just before he shoved me.

We flew from Los Angeles to Peru and boarded the riverboat. I'm not sure of much else. There's something I'm forgetting. I can feel it like a piece of popcorn stuck between two molars. I worry at the spot with my tongue, coaxing it out, seeking relief and unable to leave it alone until it's out.

What is it?

I feel the poke of the needle and the searing burn of the surgical thread passing through my skin. I stare at the white wall in front of me, feeling Steve's presence in the room even though I can't see him. His eyes bore holes into me, or maybe that's just in my mind, but I swear I can feel his gaze on my back, tracing the lines of his handprints. I dread being alone with him. The nurse can't leave.

My breath quickens.

"My name is Helene," she says. I only nod, unable to form a coherent sentence. "I'm sorry for the discomfort," Helene says. A word, along with *pressure*, that doctors and dentists use as a euphemism for actual pain. The needle feels huge and the split in my scalp is raw and tender. It feels like the thread zips through the needle hole, singeing my flesh with its speed. With each stitch, I grow more acutely aware that Helene is going to be done soon.

Thinking back on the last few days, I search for what might have happened before I went overboard. Did we get into a fight? We never fight. Our marriage is almost boring with how little conflict we have with each other. The beginning of our marriage blazed hot, though.

Passion can only take you so far. It burns fast and bright, but God, it's like heroin. Instantly addictive, coursing through your veins and making the edges of your vision fuzzy. Everything takes on a pink glow. You don't see the red flags that you should.

Helene tugs at the thread running through my skin. It burns as it moves against the wound. Squinting my eyes, I grind my teeth until they squeak against each other and I'm afraid I might crack a tooth.

Forcing myself to relax, I slow my breathing, still aware that Steve is just behind me.

What happens now?

How do we proceed?

Do I roll over and ask him why he shoved me off the boat?

Do I run? *Where?* I can't.

Everything is fuzzy. I only remember the feeling of two palms against my back. Hot, someone else's blood flowing near the surface of them as they contacted my skin, and a little damp with the sheen of sweat that's unavoidable in the Amazon.

A memory comes to me like lightning striking the tin roof of a barn.

It's the moment when I struck my head against the edge of the lower deck before I hit the water. I heard the thud before I felt it, and the impact rocked my brain inside my skull. I'm lucky to be alive, I realize.

There's something else.

Something brushed against my leg in the murky water as I sank.

Scales. Mass. The threat of ancient muscle.

I try not to think about what it was, even though I know. I'm overcome by the idea that I should make sure something didn't bite me.

"Do I have any bites?" I croak as Helene works on my scalp.

Her hands are still, shocked by the sound coming out of me.

"You don't. You're alright," she says. "I looked when they brought you onto the deck. You are lucky. A woman once fell, and the caiman got to her before we could."

I'm dazed by everything, unsure if she's joking or being serious.

Steve doesn't laugh, but I hear him sigh.

The same way he sighed when I gave him an ultimatum.

Leave her or lose me.

That was a lifetime ago. Jane's ghost dances at the edge of my mind. The wife before me. The wife I stole from. Our love was born out of deceit and our trust has always been brittle.

I don't want to roll over to face him, but before I know it, Helene tells me she's done and rolls me onto my back. I glue my eyes on the ceiling until he moves into my field of vision, craning his neck out over the table and leaning so close that I smell his breath. My heart stops.

I hear Helene fussing with instruments on a counter against the opposite wall. I need to scream. He's going to finish the job right now.

Finally, he speaks, his hot breath fanning across my face.

"My God, you could have died," he breathes.

I exhale as he leans in and wraps his arms around me. Steve hugs me tight, pulling me up from the cot and my body goes limp. Dead weight in his arms, I hang there like a rag doll. Partially because I'm probably in shock. Partially because sometimes animals play dead to evade a predator.

And right now I feel like prey.

TWO

STEVE PULLS BACK, the heat of his body growing more distant by the millisecond. It's a relief, though he squeezes my hand. Am I supposed to squeeze back? Is that a gesture of loving kindness? His fear made tangible that I might have died?

Perhaps in the moment I went overboard, he realized his error. A crime of passion, he would have called it to the Peruvian authorities. For a second, I imagine Steve in a South American prison, growing skinnier and skinnier as time passes, looking like a victim of a wasting disease at the turn of the twentieth century.

I inhale sharply and try to gather my wits. The back of my head pulses at the site of the incision and I know a headache is coming. A big one. Soon, I won't be able to think of anything else.

Helene finishes with her instruments and walks back over to the cot, placing a hand on my arm. Her skin is cool despite having worn gloves only a minute ago.

"I will get you a blanket so you can warm up," she tells me. "And let's get you out of that dress. Could your husband get you something to wear?"

She turns to him when she asks, giving him a stern look, as though he'd better do as she says. I imagine Helene has taken charge of several crises in her day, even though she seems to be barely thirty.

Steve nods, almost frantically, and stumbles over his words.

"Yes, yes. Of course. I'll be right back."

The thick tension in the room loosens as soon as he disappears into the dark corridor. I let out a shaky breath.

"Do you remember what happened?" Helene asks.

I roll my head to face her. I try to shake it but instantly regret it. The ache is setting in.

"No," I whisper.

Helene's brow furrows as she stares me down. Younger than me by a decade, her presence is the most imposing I've encountered in a while. I don't imagine people lie to her often.

"I don't remember anything," I reiterate. "Nothing but feeling something in the water brushing against my leg."

"Anaconda," Helene says. "We spotted it just as we pulled you from the river."

This information would shock me if it was the only devastating piece of news I was trying to process. But it's not, and because of that, it goes into one ear like radio static and leaves the other as a wisp of ether. *Anaconda, you say? One of those great enormous snakes? Ha! How strange.*

But everything feels strange.

I sit up and Helene places a hand on my shoulder. Her touch is gentle, but firm, just like her demeanor. Helene probably never raises her voice. I don't think anyone would be silly enough to push her to that point. I do as she's telling me and lean back onto the cot.

"This is very important, Mrs. Silkwood," she says softly. "What happened that caused you to fall overboard?"

My mind screams *him! It was him! My husband! Who else could it be? Don't let him back in! Please!*

"I don't know," I tell her.

Maybe it's the fact that we're on a riverboat sailing down the Amazon, trapped in close proximity to each other. Maybe it's a misplaced loyalty I feel to Steve. Maybe it's that I'm stupid. But for whatever reason, I suddenly understand every woman I've heard about on the news who won't press charges against her abuser.

I can't bring myself to say it out loud.

That will make his betrayal real.

That will make me a victim.

And how would Steve react?

He's already tried to kill me once.

I feel Helene's eyes against my skin, white hot and burning holes through me.

"You can tell me, Mrs. Silkwood," she says, her voice almost so reassuring that I do.

Saying nothing, I just look at her, wondering what Helene's story is. How she came to be on this boat.

"What happened to the woman with the caiman?" I ask.

"They tore her apart. Bit off her arm, she bled into the river. Tiny maroon waves lapped at the back deck of the boat." She never breaks eye contact with me as she speaks. "She was a beautiful woman. Looked a little bit like you, in fact. On vacation with her husband and two teenage sons. Do you have children, Mrs. Silkwood?"

"No," I say.

"Why not?"

It's a question you grow less uncomfortable with as you age in your decision not to breed. Somehow, though, the people asking seem to be just as horrified every time you answer.

"I don't want children. I never did," I tell her. "My husband did. My first husband, I mean." I find myself unable to stop babbling. "Steve doesn't, though. Neither of us wants children. Plus, I'm forty now. It would be a big risk."

I've been tacking my age on to the end of my response for five years. Ever since I could qualify as a geriatric preg-nancy. The science is behind me! They can't argue with that unless they want to outwardly say a woman becoming a mother is more important than that woman's health and safety. Most people find that easier to swallow, thinking that I just missed my window of opportunity. *Poor Stephanie.*

"You're smart," Helene says, surprising me.

"I would say lucky," I say with a smile that surprises me. "I wasn't the most careful when I was younger. Thinking I was invincible and all of that."

"Apparently you are," she says.

I blink, confused.

"You hit your head very hard." She brings me back to the present moment. "Hard enough that you should be dead."

She pierces me with that gaze again, hoping to burrow under my skin and get me to confess whatever it is she thinks I know.

But I don't know anything.

Do I?

I have a memory of being pushed. But I was looking out at the jungle, I realize. It comes to me quickly, the vision of the tree canopy. I hear the shriek of a howler monkey from somewhere deep in the jungle. Their calls can be heard up to three miles away. I remember reading that before the trip. That thought came to me just before I was shoved. When it happened, I wasn't expecting it.

Had I thought I was alone?

I realize then that there's no visual memory of who was with me in those final moments. But it had to be Steve. Why would it be anyone else?

"What time is it?" I ask Helene.

"Near midnight," she says.

"Knock, knock," Steve says softly as he enters the room, tapping twice on the open door. I stiffen and find myself scared once again, but he smiles gently at me. Over his arm are pajama pants and a soft t-shirt of his that I love. I didn't realize he had packed it. I'm the only one that ever wears it anymore.

"Thought you might like this." He touches the shirt, seeing me looking at it.

"Thank you," I manage, though my voice has grown softer.

"She alright?" Steve turns to Helene and places the clothes on the end of the cot.

"I'd like to observe her for the night," Helene says. "Just to be sure. But she is stable."

He nods, biting his lower lip.

"Did she say anything about what happened?" He asks softly, as though it's a secret. As though I'm a child and he's talking to the principal after having been called straight from work to deal with my misbehavior.

Helene casts a disapproving glance at me and then looks back at Steve.

"She remembers nothing." There's a note of frustration in Helene's voice. She sighs and crosses her arms.

"Can I stay with her?" Steve asks.

Helene glances at me once more and reads the unblinking dread on my face in a split second.

"There's no need. I'd prefer it if she was undisturbed tonight. I'll keep an eye on her," she says, that stern command of the conversation returning.

Even Steve, CEO of a print-on-demand merchandising business and multi-millionaire, forty-five and unaccustomed to being told what to do, listens attentively to this young woman and only nods in agreement.

"I will let you know if anything changes," she says. "I think she should rest now."

The last sentence has a finality to it. The conversation is over. She's telling him to leave, and he understands. He nods again and then steps over, squeezing my hand and smiling down at me.

"You'll be just fine," he says. "You've always been a survivor."

His mouth quirks up at the corner. He lets go of my hand, and right then, I'm not sure if that was a smirk or a sneer.

THREE

WE WERE *both married when we met.*

You to her, and me to him. Both of us trying to project happiness to the outside world.

I remember the party where it happened. A large gathering for a cocktail hour that would inevitably meander into the wee hours of the morning. Everyone was dressed in their sexiest, yet still elegant, clothing. The women wore five-inch heels and dresses they couldn't bend over in. The men had tailored three-piece suits that made each of them look like a different delicacy.

You were no exception.

I clocked you when you arrived. Tall. Taller than my husband by at least two inches and he was 6'2". Built like an athlete, your suit hugged your muscular arms. Gray with a purple tie that popped right out. And then I saw her join you at the threshold. She took your arm, and you smiled at her. There was a tenderness in the expression.

The way you might look at a favorite niece or nephew. I wondered if she was your date.

I estimated that you were in your mid-thirties. Young, hungry, and looking for all possible networking opportunities tonight. Sipping my champagne, I remembered a time when my husband was just like you. The thought of him made me glance over my shoulder, scanning the room for him.

Finally, after a second pass, I spotted him near the grand piano, clapping the back of some other businessman after a joke that was undoubtedly hilarious. I downed the rest of my glass and grabbed another as a waiter passed by. I offered him a smile, glad he wasn't the same waiter that I had gotten my first two glasses from.

A headache would come in the morning, but these things were unbearable without a little social lubricant.

"Stephanie! How are you?"

I spun, mid-sip, and spotted Ray Greenwood. My husband's biggest client. We'd met before, and Ray had always given me the creeps. He was surrounded by no less than three beautiful women tonight who barely looked legal. Just another piece of data to add to the pile of his growing slime factor.

He embraced me before I said a word, hugging me far too tightly for far too long. His hands lingered at my waist when he let go of me.

"Where's your hubby?" Ray asked.

I glanced back at the grand piano, but he was gone. Of course. Like the police in a Netflix true crime special, he was never there when I needed him.

"He's around here somewhere," I said with a big fake smile.

"You look gorgeous as ever," Ray said. I could smell his breath and I fought the urge to make a face. I pulled back and placed a hand on his chest, creating some distance between us.

"Who are your lovely companions?" I asked, trying to turn Ray's attention back to the teenagers he brought here with him tonight. "And did their parents sign permission slips?"

Ray thought it was a good-natured joke.

He always did.

Insulting him was easy. He was a caricature of an aging millennial searching for meaning as an influencer. He dated women that were far too young for him because women his age would never put up with him. Whether Ray found any meaning in his life as a content creator is up for debate, but he was filthy rich. And like most other filthy rich men, he thought nothing was off limits. Including me.

"Good one," he said with a snicker. "Let me introduce you. This is Haley, Brinley, and Max," he said, pointing to each of them.

"And they're all...your dates?"

"Be more progressive than that, Steph," he said, chastising me. "My love is big, and it needs a lot of room to...stretch out, if you know what I mean." He winked.

I most assuredly did know what he meant, and it had nothing to do with love. Ray thought with his penis and it had led him into several questionable business *decisions, the last of which he almost didn't recover from.*

I took a large swig of champagne.

"Sure," I said with a forced smile.

Ray stared talking and suddenly it was like I was hearing Charlie Brown's teacher, muffled by the sound of silverware and glass clanking, along with voices mingling louder and louder to be heard above the crowd. I just nodded when he paused, hoping it was the appropriate time.

"What do you think?" he asked.

I pulled away, suddenly aware that I hadn't paid attention to anything he'd said. I stared at him for a moment like a deer in the headlights.

"There you are!"

I spun and saw a man. It was you. The man I'd been staring at earlier. I'm sure shock registered on my face.

"I've been looking for you all over," you said. "You'll have to excuse us," you said to Ray. "I need to talk to Stephanie about some important business."

You tugged me gently by the arm, and I followed you gratefully. Ray looked like he'd just been bamboozled out of a thousand dollars. He turned to his companions for comfort, his face sullen.

"Thank you," I said, the words gushing out. "Thank you so much."

"Well, I know what it's like to be cornered by Ray Greenwood, and I can only imagine what it's like as a woman," you said. You did a playful shudder.

"That's about right," I said with a smile.

Your gaze lingered, both of us looking at each other. I felt butterflies in my stomach and broke the stare. I laughed and took a sip of champagne.

"Well, I'll leave you to it," I said.

"Not so fast," you said. "Ray's watching. We might as well get to know each other or he'll be onto us."

I glanced over at Ray. Even though his dates were trying to comfort him, Ray's mood seemed irretrievable.

"Right," I said.

We exchanged pleasantries. You were charming. More charming than anyone I'd ever met. A quality that I was sure spelled danger the moment I recognized it. But like a bug zapper's light to a moth, I was drawn closer to that hazardous glow and unable to look away.

"Is that woman you were with your date?" I asked, taking a sip of champagne.

Your smile faltered.

"Wife," you said.

But the way you said it made me think you wished you didn't have to. Like we were sharing a little secret that no one else in the world knew. You wished you'd come here alone tonight.

Your eyes found mine and something passed between us, unspoken. The heat of it was blistering. Pure desire. I looked away and felt a blush rush to my cheeks.

"Congratulations," I said when I looked up, managing to conjure the most idiotic statement I could.

You chuckled.

"Thank you," you said. And then you toasted my glass.

"It's been lovely to talk to you Stephanie," you told me. I nodded.

"Lovely," I repeated, the word hanging between us for a moment.

You turned and walked away. You were gone into the crowd, just like that.

And so was that feeling of floating.

I knew then that I was doomed.

FOUR

WITH THE HELP OF A SEDATIVE, I sleep through the night. My head throbs the moment I open my eyes, even though the room is dark. Turning onto my elbow, I cast a glance around the room. Dim light from the hallway pours in through the open door, and I find Helene sitting on a stool at the counter, a paperback novel in her hands with a little book light illuminating her face from below.

"What are you reading?" I ask, even though the effort of speaking sends jolts of pain down my neck and across my temples.

"Good morning," Helene says, closing her book. "It's *How to Change Your Mind* by Michael Pollan."

I vaguely recognize the title, probably from an article I caught scrolling through Facebook. I don't recall much else about it, though.

"Does your head hurt?" Helene asks.

"Massively," I say with a sigh, closing my eyes as though that might alleviate the pain. It doesn't.

"Here," Helene says. I open my eyes just a bit and watch her turn, grabbing something from the cabinet above her. A prescription pill bottle, it looks like. She shakes out two pills and hands them to me without water. "The sink is there," she points to the wall ahead of me, then helps pull me into a sitting position. I gratefully take the pills with a handful of water without asking what they are. A painkiller I assume, and hopefully the opioid variety. I don't think Advil will solve this one.

"Thank you," I say, turning in the darkness and leaning against the sink.

For a moment, my mind is blissfully clear. Nothing behind me, nothing before me, only this moment in the darkened infirmary room.

It's a flash in the pan, lasting no longer than three seconds. Immediately, I think of Steve. Then I think of last night, and all that I can't remember. A huge dark hole of nothingness. Anything could fill it. All manner of terrors start to creep in at the edges of this particular mental picture.

I think of the look on Steve's face last night. The smirk turned sneer.

"Are you ready to go back to your room?" Helene asks. "Your husband has been asking for you."

The last sentence is weighted. She's giving me another opportunity to come clean and tell her what I know. I wish I could.

"Yes," I say.

At least the ache in my head will provide a distraction from the uneasiness I feel about going back to the room. About being alone with my husband. What a strange thought.

"I'll walk you," Helene says, almost like she fears I won't make it there without her.

I just nod.

We go up to the second deck. There are ten rooms on this floor and ten rooms on the first. Ours happens to be number thirteen. Lucky or unlucky, depending on who you ask. We don't have the key, so Helene knocks. And as though Steve's been waiting, doorknob in hand, this whole time, he answers it instantly.

"I was just coming to check on you," he says.

"She has a pretty bad headache, but she'll be alright. I recommend she rest as much as she can."

Steve turns his focus to Helene, seemingly having to rip his eyes away from me. Like he's sizing me up, wondering exactly what I've told Helene in the hours we've spent together.

"Good, good," Steve says, repeating the word the second time as though to reassure himself.

He looks at me, then. The devastation that was on his face last night is gone, replaced by something stonier. I don't know how to gauge it. What emotion is he feeling? There's a wall between us. I can feel it all the way out here.

"I'll leave you two, then," Helene says. She looks at

me one last time, like she's saying *last chance!* I turn away, tempted by her determination, but I have nothing to tell her. Still.

She disappears down the small staircase that twists on itself to reach the first level of the riverboat. I watch until she's out of sight.

"How are you?" Steve asks.

"I'm okay," I say, sounding more unsure of myself than I have in a while. That note in my voice reminds me of the early days of our marriage, when I still worried if I could trust him. That horrible anxious feeling like all the butterflies in my stomach had ceased to fly, dead under the weight of intuition.

I feel the rumblings of that now. For an entirely different reason.

What if he *did* push me?

"Good," he says. He steps aside, motioning for me to come into the room. I do as I'm instructed.

Things look as I remember them from our first night on the boat. The bed is neatly made. Someone must have come by. Steve would never do that on his own. I sit down on the edge of it, looking out the window as the jungle passes us by, slow and steady. The exact opposite of the rhythm my heart is beating out in my chest. I'm scared Steve might hear it rattling the cage of my ribs.

"It's beautiful," I say, sounding like someone making small talk at one of those awful cocktail parties.

"You picked a good vacation," he says.

"Do you…" I find myself broaching the question, even though I know I shouldn't. But I can't stand it. I can't stand being in this room with him, bearing the weight of my assumptions about what happened last night. "Do you know what happened to me last night?" I ask.

I look over at him.

His face tightens slightly, worry lines forming between his brows.

"You don't remember?" he asks.

He sounds concerned, but I remind myself he's a man who lied to his first wife about his whereabouts for over a year without getting caught.

I shake my head in a jerky motion, feeling more vulnerable than I did the night I told him I was in love.

Steve kneels in front of me, taking my hand.

"You fell," he says.

A white-hot jolt of fear dumps into my veins.

I can *feel* his hands against my back. *Force* pushed me overboard.

"How?"

My voice is barely a whisper. A tear spills onto my cheek, and he wipes it away with his thumb. His hand lingers at my chin.

"You were just too close to the edge, darling," he says.

I swallow and I'm sure he can hear the bolus in my throat bobbing up and down inside my neck. My mouth is dry. Suddenly, a memory comes to me. The month before we left for South America, we fought constantly. It was so unlike us. Things had been more tense than ever in our marriage. Both of us were on edge and I struggle to bring to mind *why*. All of it seems so silly now.

Was it worth killing me over?

Something that huge would be seared into my memory. I'm sure of it.

"I can't believe I was so careless," I say. My words come out softly, his hand still against my face.

"You'll be more careful next time," he says.

There's something in his tone. The hint of a threat. It stills my heart for a split second. I'm standing in the jaws of a giant black caiman, not having realized I'd wandered in on mistake. And now I'm trapped.

"I will," I assure him.

He lets his hand fall, but he remains kneeling in front of me.

"Collin and Cece want to see you," he says.

The names are instantly familiar, but when I try to bring the people they represent to the forefront of my mind, I'm met with only fuzzy vagueness. Two shapes. Male and female. Our friends. But nothing else.

"Oh," I say.

Panic floods my extremities, making me feel like I weigh ten tons and I weigh nothing at the same time. Like my soul could leave my body right now.

I struggle to remember them. Anything about them. Times we've spent together. There are flashes, here and there, hazy as my first memories of childhood, characterized only by shapes and colors and a cloudy recollection of location.

"I'll go get them and let them know you're back," Steve says. He stands and heads for the door. "They've been worried about you," he says as he steps out into the hallway and closes the door.

I think about locking it.

About hiding.

It's no use. We're stuck here.

And I'm about to meet two people that I should know everything about.

FIVE

I'M SO STILL and silent that I hear Steve's retreating footfalls as he walks down the hallway and knocks on the cabin door next to ours. When I jump at the muffled thumps, I force myself to breathe slowly, intentionally. I'm getting that feeling of disconnect with my body, like at any moment I could float away. It's the panic.

I steel my nerves and remind myself I've been in tough situations. When I married my first husband, I was dancing at Racy's Gentlemen's Club for money. Herschel was older, lonely. I was young, beautiful, and being paid to listen as he waxed poetic about his deceased wife. I often wondered if I would ever be as lucky as he'd been. Great loss means there was great love. And at that point in my life, I hadn't yet experienced a great love, though I'd known plenty of loss.

Herschel promised he would take care of me, and he did. He got me out of there. But it was excruciating. I realized how much of my life I was missing out on. All my friends that still worked at the club were having the adventures you're meant to in your twenties. I was playing arm candy to Herschel.

I would mingle with the men he did business with and make sure they knew he'd gotten a prize.

Steve had already written the story of Herschel's second broken heart before he laid a single finger on me.

Herschel didn't live much longer after I left him. I've always carried that and felt like I had betrayed him on a level deeper than romantic love.

Steve was an escape from the monotony of safety. I thought then that he might be my great love.

I think about how simple things were before I left Racy's to become a wife. Hard, but simple.

I survived back then. Before Steve. Before Herschel. I can survive this.

No one was trying to kill you at Racy's. And you could leave that place.

Hard, but simple.

I just have to last long enough that I can get off this boat and away from Steve.

Voices echo outside in the hallway and my gut knots. The moment of truth is almost here.

How well can I sell this?

I think about all the nights I put on a performance at Racy's. Not the dancing, but the listening. Being whatever they needed me to be in that moment. Pretending I'd never even *think* of being anywhere else.

I can do this.

And surely, after a moment, something will jog my

memory and these people's involvement in our lives will come back to me. Their identities will come back to me.

Just as I assure myself of this, a knock rattles our door and I jump, startled even though I'm expecting them.

"Come in," I call, trying to project a brightness in my voice. The pain medication is beginning to kick in. I feel the ache in my skull become muted and distant. The only disadvantage is that I also feel the sharpness of my mind become dulled.

Steve opens the door and steps inside. Two people follow him.

Surprising myself, I'm slightly relieved that Steve's with us.

The woman is so much shorter than me at about 5'3". Her husband, on the other hand, is huge. They both have sandy blonde hair, hers falling to her waist and his falling in soft curls at his neck, looking like a prime vacation coiffing.

Both of them look like they've taken advantage of all the tanning opportunities we've had in the last two days. I wonder if they were tan before we left Los Angeles. A stone sinks in my gut as I realize I have no idea.

The woman stands next to her husband, arms crossed. I make eye contact, telling myself to hold it as though I know her. I force a smile and she seems to force one in return. I wonder what her hesitation is, and realize the whole thing has probably put something of a wet blanket on the whole trip. I feel compelled to speak.

"Well, I'm alright," I say with a tiny chuckle. It's hollow and I hope they don't detect that about it.

Her husband cracks an awkward smile. Hers grows more warm.

"We're glad you're alright. Collin was sick," she glances at her husband. "I was, too. Such a shock. Are you really alright?"

"I'm fine," I assure her, trying to take as much command of the conversation as I can. "I'm sure you've both been worried. Steve was, too."

I glance at him. He nods, as though brought back to the present by the brief pause where we all look to him to see his reaction to my words.

"Too much excitement for me," Steve offers with a pressed smile. "Cece, do you want to sit?"

He gestures to Collin's wife.

She looks like a Cece. A small name for a small woman. I dread standing up next to her at 5'11". Short women make me so self-conscious of my height. Between Steve, Collin, and myself, Cece will look like a teenager.

Cece takes a seat in a chair in the corner of the room, crossing her legs at her ankles and wrapping her hands around her tan knee. Collin hovers at the door with Steve, hands in his pockets.

A thought occurs to me.

Either of them could have seen something.

It washes over me like a bucket of ice water dumped over my head. Anyone in this room could have a piece of information that would bring me closer to knowing exactly what happened last night.

One of them more so than the others.

I glance at Steve when silence falls on the group of

us. He seems lost in thought, unaware of the awkward-ness in the room. If this were a dinner party at our house, I'd prod him to interact. Now, I don't feel like I should do anything to agitate him.

I glance at Collin, making eye contact with him. I offer a smile.

The corner of his mouth tugs up somewhat nervously. Almost like he's not sure how he should act in the situation. I don't blame him. But then his eyes dart away, almost like he's afraid that if I look at him too long, I might read his mind.

He looks to Cece, then looks down. I glance at her and her eyes feel mine, meeting them. She smiles as though nothing about this situation is strange.

My God. They know something.

Another horrible realization washes over me.

Not only *could* these people know something about what happened to me, but they *do*.

SIX

I KNEW *we would have an affair the day I met you at Starbucks in Los Angeles.*

He'd sent me to meet you and hand off a new client file. Someone that you'd already established a relationship with. It had been the subject of your conversation the night he hired you. The night of that dreadful cocktail party. You were quite the salesman.

I spotted you instantly when I walked in.

Tall, leaning against the wall, waiting for a drink and sharing a laugh with the woman behind you. I had no doubt you were charming her just as you had me. But there was something lacking in your expression towards her. You hadn't crossed any lines. I could tell just from watching the way you interacted with her. It drew a small smile to my lips, and I cleared my throat, hoping to instantly suppress it. There was something different in the way you had looked at me the night of the cocktail party.

It wasn't immediately that I knew we'd cross a line. It came later.

In the middle of chuckling at one of the woman's jokes, you turned and your eye caught mine. I smiled at you, almost like we were sharing a secret. Your performative smile shifted in favor of something less programmed. Something warmer.

I couldn't help but smile in return, and as soon as I realized it, I looked away. You brought that out in me. Something I hadn't done for a long time. Something that I'd reserved for men at the club all that time ago. It felt distant, ancient. This primal feminine part of me that recognized you as a man who knew what he wanted, whether he said it in words or not.

I could feel it. Even then, across the room with thirty other people next to us. In that moment, you only had eyes for me. You stared so long, the woman next to you shifted her gaze to see what had distracted you. I glanced at her for a moment and offered a smile, feeling like she was on to us. Like she knew we shouldn't be looking at each other like that.

He shouldn't have sent me on this errand.

Maybe it was his fault, after all.

For so long, I blamed myself, but things had been tough. Things hadn't been like they were in the beginning. He was still kind, and I still loved him, but there was something about you that excited a part of me I thought was long gone.

The barista called out your name, and you stepped up to get your order, then made a beeline straight for me.

"Not many open tables in here," you remarked as you held your steaming Americano. I'd heard the barista call out your order.

It was too hot for that, but somehow, you remained cool. Always, I would come to learn.

"No, there aren't," I say. "I'm not going to stay, though." I added the last as if it had only just occurred to me.

"Won't you have some coffee with me?" You held my gaze for a moment longer than necessary. "Who knows when we might get the opportunity again?" You paused. "As busy as we are." The last was added as an afterthought. A disclaimer. A note, so that anyone listening wouldn't suspect either of our intentions.

"I really shouldn't," I said with a smile, holding out the client folder to you.

But you didn't take it.

I held it there, out in the air between us. You looked down at it, a smirk turning up the corner of your mouth.

"I insist," you said. "Indulge me and I'll let you be on your way."

You smiled at me warmly. It was the kind of smile that held an invitation. Like you were asking me to be part of your life, even though we were just having coffee.

Your charm was devastating. Even for a woman used to men charming their way into her bed.

"Fine," I said. As if I had a choice.

I'd known from the moment we met that I didn't. There was no decision made. It was fate. From that moment, we'd been set on a collision course that would end my marriage, and yours. At least two people would be left in the wreckage. All I could comfort myself with was the thought that looking into your eyes made me forget both of them.

It's so dangerous to meet someone like you. Someone who can erase any sense of obligation or ethics. I wondered if it was like that for you, too. And later you'd tell me it was. That you'd known the moment you saw me. You'd been planning to come talk to me all evening. And as soon as you realized I was going to be meeting you at Starbucks, you'd decided you had to make me stay.

"What would you like?" you asked, looking back at the counter. The line had thinned and most people were working away on their laptops or joining a friend to catch up. Even the woman that had been waiting at the counter behind you had just disappeared out the front door, onward to her next adventure.

"Really, I don't need anything," I told you.

There was a part of me that felt trepidation. A part of me that knew if I stayed for this one conversation, it meant a lot more than that.

"Just a water," I acquiesced with a smile.

Water never hurt anyone.

Especially not filtered water.

You grabbed me a bottle of Ethos in a flash and paid for it before I could insist that was unnecessary.

"A business expense," you teased, waving it away with your hand as if it meant nothing.

For a split second, I hoped you were being truthful about that. For a split second, the life I had come to know flashed before my eyes. I knew I was putting it in danger by even entertaining the idea of you. It only took a couple more steps for that to become more than a fantasy, and sitting down to have coffee certainly seemed like one of those steps to me.

"There's a table on the patio," you said.

I followed you out there. The weather was nice. Cool, but still the earliest part of fall. Neither of us had a jacket, nor did we need one. The people around us were lost in their own conversations or nose burrowed deep in computer work with AirPods burrowed just as deep in their ear canals.

It felt safe.

Like for a moment, nothing else existed. We were just two people innocently having coffee.

I placed the file on the table and pushed it toward you. You only leaned back in your chair, taking a sip of your drink that I imagined was still too hot. You grimaced and made a sound of satisfaction, making me think I was right. Maybe you were one of those people that liked it when their coffee almost burned their mouth.

The thought amused me, and I chuckled.

"What is it?" you asked, a smile on your lips now, too.

"Nothing. I just—" I cut myself off. "Nothing." I smiled and opened my water, taking a sip.

"Oh, come on. What was it?" you teased.

"It just looked like you might have gotten a sip that was a little too hot," I said.

"Never." You feigned a manliness in your voice. "Real men don't get scalded by hot beverages. Don't you know

that?" You smiled and leaned forward on the table. "Actually, you're right. Was it that obvious? I think I have a blister now."

I chuckled.

"That's what I get for trying to be cool," you said with a smile.

"Why were you trying to be cool?" I asked.

The words were out of my mouth before I could stop them.

I blushed looking at you. Your eyes lingered on mine, your mouth slightly parted in a smile.

You knew. So did I.

You cleared your throat, like common sense had finally returned to you after a long absence.

"I suppose I should take this," you said, finally reaching for the file folder.

I smiled, wishing you'd taken it to begin with. But there was also a part of me that wanted this to continue. A twinge of sadness that your good judgment might have gotten the better of you.

"I should go," I told you.

I stood from the table.

"But thank you for the water," I said.

You stood.

"Let me walk you to your car," you offered.

I knew I should turn you down, but I didn't. You followed me out into the parking lot. Afternoon sun beat down on it, right there in the open. Anyone could have seen what happened next.

Maybe that was part of why it was so thrilling.

Maybe that was what hooked me.

Maybe on some level, we both wanted to get caught.

I turned just as I reached the car to say goodbye to you.

And you kissed me.

Your hands were on my face before I could blurt out any protest, and I wouldn't have, even if I'd had the time.

You pulled away and looked into my eyes.

"Well," you said, stepping back and straightening your shirt. I did the same.

"I—" I tried to articulate something—what, I wasn't sure.

"Until next time," you said with a smirk.

And it wasn't until you had disappeared around the building that I realized I was smiling right back at you.

SEVEN

WE ALL AGREE to go downstairs and enjoy the scenery as the riverboat sails onward, further into the rainforest. It's not at all lost on me that civilization is a long way away. Whatever happens, I need to keep my wits about me and my head above water, figuratively and literally, until it's not quite so far from us.

Preferably until I set foot on solid ground again.

After that, I'm not sure what's going to happen.

Surviving the cruise is all that's on my mind right now.

I change before heading downstairs and Steve waits for me. I emerge from the bathroom in linen pants and a deep green tank top. I thought about putting on a necklace, but it occurred to me that someone could grab it, use it as leverage.

The thought is grotesque, macabre. Not at all the kind of thought I imagined I'd be having on vacation.

But here we are. Deep into the belly of the Amazon, stuck with each other.

And I don't know if I can trust any of them.

I force a smile at Steve, hoping to ease any concern he might have about what I do and don't remember from last night.

"You look beautiful," he says.

There's something wistful in his tone. Almost a sadness.

"You say that like it's a bad thing," I venture.

"Just reminds me of when we first met," he offers a smile that doesn't quite reach his eyes.

"You mean when we started having an affair?" The words are out there in the room between us, my filter apparently on vacation, too.

He looks at me, and for a moment, his face is expressionless. I struggle to read what's going on behind his eyes. And then he smiles.

"We didn't really start things on the best foot, did we?" He offers a little chuckle.

"It worked out anyway," I say, making my face a blank canvas, letting him project whatever he wants onto it. I give him a neutral smile.

"It did," he says.

He reaches for me and pulls me toward him. I allow it and he wraps his arms around my waist, resting his head just below my sternum as he hugs me. Listening, I think briefly, for any indication that I know something I shouldn't.

I place my hands on his face, summoning up every ounce of *good wife* that I can.

"I'm fine, Steve," I assure him, pretending that I think any disturbance in his mood is based out of worry for my well-being.

"Are you sure?" He's convincing. His brow furrows and his eyes search mine.

"I'm fine," I tell him again. "Just a little banged up. That's all."

I smile down at him, then take his hands and pull him into a standing position.

"We should go," I say.

He nods and follows me out into the hallway. He locks the door behind us with the single key we were given when we boarded the boat. It's a green, old school motel-style keychain with the name of the riverboat cruising company on it, along with our room number, and their slogan. *The trip of a lifetime.*

They got that right.

I follow Steve down the narrow staircase that leads us to the main deck. There are several arrangements of couches and chairs for visiting or playing board games or cards. At the far end of the area is a little bar. It's tempting to go get a drink, but I'm not sure it would be the wisest thing I could do right now. The head injury and the pain medication probably wouldn't mix well with alcohol.

Not to mention the fact that I already can't remember anything about our companions. A fact that Steve is blissfully unaware of.

It's something I have to keep to myself. If he knew that, he'd have the upper hand for sure.

He could fill my head with anything. Right now, I'm *tabula rasa*. A blank slate and susceptible to any suggestion. I need to guard my mind.

None of them can know.

Steve offers to bring me water from the bar, obviously thinking the same thing I was about the pain medication and the injury. I nod and thank him and take a seat on one of the leather loveseats that faces another. I lean back, trying to relax and look out at the rainforest passing us by. I notice two caimans on the bank, sunning.

I think about the scales that brushed my leg last night. How easily Helene identified it as an anaconda. They'd seen it swim past just after. The thought is horrifying to a woman who grew up in Los Angeles. The most fearsome creature I ever worried about was a coyote that became brave enough to raid the dumpster at my apartment complex.

Of course, mountain lions are a threat in Los Angeles. At least on the trails.

A memory comes to me. Our first night on the boat. Overhearing a conversation between a man and his new wife. He looked to be in his sixties and she in her twenties, leading me to assume the main reason she found herself on the boat had to do with his bank account.

He was telling her about his life as a hunter, regaling her with wonderful tales about predators he'd overcome during his heyday.

He mentioned the jaguars that live here. He talked

about how deadly they are. That they can sneak right up on you and break your neck before you even realize you're not alone.

An unpleasant visual comes to mind.

"Here you go," Steve says, handing me a bottle of water.

"Not very eco-conscious for a jungle cruise," I remark.

"I'd say not," he says with a smile in his voice.

He sounds more like the man I married. For a moment, it sets me at ease. Like this is just another trip. Like nothing bad has happened and in a few days, we'll just be on a flight home to Los Angeles to get on with our busy lives.

I wonder if I made it up.

What if it's all in my head? The thought of the hands against my back. The feeling of being shoved. Maybe no one was acting weird upstairs. Maybe I was just reading it all through a lens that was telling me something's up when it's not.

I've never been unsure of myself like this before.

"You alright?" Steve's voice penetrates my thoughts.

"Fine," I say, a little too quickly and brightly. He gives me a look, telling me he knows better, but just as he's opening his mouth to say something to me about it, Collin and Cece join us.

"There you are," Collin says to the two of us.

"I'm sure it was a struggle to find us," Steve teases.

Collin laughs and Cece smiles. I smile back and she holds my gaze.

I'm struck again by that feeling that everyone here is trying to read my mind.

I look away, shaking it off and telling myself I'm losing it.

The memory floods over me. Being shoved from the boat. The feeling of those hot palms against my skin. It's unmistakable. If I made that up, I have a hell of a lot better imagination than I thought I did.

I glance back at Cece and she's got her hands clasped in her lap. She has such delicate hands. I glance at my own. Fingers long and not so slender. More like a man's hands. Something that likely comes with the territory of being almost six feet tall. For a moment, I'm irritated that they came with us. Things would be much less complicated if they hadn't.

"What's on the agenda for the evening?" Collin asks.

"No stops tonight," Steve says. "Just cruising. Dinner, it looks like. Try not to fall overboard this time." he says to me.

He's joking, I know, but it catches me off guard. It's darker than his usual humor. Maybe that's his way of coping with almost having lost me. Or maybe he's upset that his shove didn't finish me off. Maybe it's a threat.

I swallow and smile, aware of every inch of my body under the scrutiny of his gaze.

He claps me on the thigh, and squeezes as he talks to Collin. Is it my imagination, or is he squeezing just a little too tight?

"What are they serving for dinner tonight?" I ask Cece.

"Sea bass, I think," she says.

Like lightning, a memory strikes me.

"I'm sure you'd prefer if it were Mahi Mahi," I say, offering her a conspiratorial smile.

Her favorite fish. The dish she gets when we all go out to our favorite restaurant in Los Angeles. I see her tiny, slender finger tapping the menu as she tells the waiter. *My absolute favorite kind of fish.*

Her eyes light up slightly. I've hit on something. My memory is right.

It rings inside my mind like a tuning fork. The truth.

I soak it in, trying to make my body remember this feeling. The way it resonates. This is what reality feels like.

Hold on to this, Stephanie. You're going to need it.

"You're right about that," Cece says with a small chuckle. "I don't really care for any other kind."

"Well, in less than a week, we'll be back in the states and you can get some," I assure her with the warmest smile I can manage. She returns it, and I find myself in another moment that feels familiar. Comfortable. Like home.

Cece and I must like each other. I wonder if we ever went to do things by ourselves. If our friendship extended beyond our husbands. I need to find out.

Cece knows something. Maybe she's afraid to say something because of Steve. Or maybe because of Collin. What if I could get her to tell me what she's holding back? What if she desperately *wants* to tell me?

Her eyes linger on mine for a moment. I will her to read my thoughts.

"How are you feeling?" she finally asks.

"I feel fine," I tell her. It's partially true. The pain medicine is doing wonders. And other than the fact that I can't remember anything about her or her husband, or the moments that led up to my almost-demise, I'm doing alright. I feel fairly normal. I smile at her.

She takes a moment to respond, almost like she's having to roll that over in her mind. Like she's not sure I'm telling the whole truth.

"Are you really?" She leans forward as she asks. The guys are lost in their own conversation.

"I am," I say.

"That was terrifying," she says. Her eyes glaze over as the memory sweeps her away. "You could have died."

I nod. The whole experience is so far away, blunted and blurry, and just a story that someone else has told me. It's not real to me. I can only imagine it. Except the part with the anaconda. That and the two hands on my back.

"It was scary," I tell her.

"Crazy thing to happen," she says. Her eyes meet mine, no longer glazed with memory. She stares intently at me for what seems like an eternity. I fight my urge to break her gaze. "Crazy," she repeats. "Well, I'm glad you're okay."

I nod, but cling to that word.

Crazy.

I think about the possibility that so much of what happened is in my mind.

The hands. The shove. What if none of that actually happened?

The anaconda could have just been in my imagination, too.

Wait.

No. It was real.

Helene *saw* the anaconda.

I smile at Cece, but say nothing.

What if *she* saw something last night?

EIGHT

STEVE AND COLLIN CONTINUE TALKING, and I catch little bits and pieces. They're on about business. Talking about this or that. Things that weren't completely taken care of before we all left town, and things that need to be taken care of the moment our wheels hit the runway in Los Angeles. The conversation turns to the trip, and just as we're discussing an upcoming hike into the jungle, a young man that works for the cruise company stops by and gently interrupts us.

"I just wanted to let you know that there is an opening for a couple's massage right at the moment. We had a cancellation. Would any of you be interested?"

He glances from Steve to Collin and back again.

Both of them shake their heads as if such a thing were ridiculous. I look at Cece and smile, raising my eyebrows. She smiles in return and gives me a little shrug. It's hardly a confirmation, but I'm going with it.

I need to get her alone.

"Cece and I are getting massages," I say proudly to the guys.

Steve immediately stops talking and turns to me.

"Are you sure that's a good idea?" he asks.

Confusion stops me from answering immediately.

"I mean, with the head injury. Could it hurt?"

"I don't think so," I tell him. "I'll ask Helene. Don't worry."

I stand up, and Cece does the same.

"Right this way," says the young man.

We follow him, heading below deck to where the spa room is, and they're ready for us. Or at least they're ready for the couple that canceled. Two women in white usher us into the massage room. Two tables are prepped and ready to go.

Cece and I step inside. The room is dimly lit with pink LED lights, and it's meant to be romantic, I'm sure. It's rather relaxing, I have to admit.

"We'll give you a moment to undress," one of the women says in the most pleasant, low tone I think I've ever heard in my life. She could narrate the dictionary and lower your blood pressure.

They step outside and Cece turns to me.

"Weren't you supposed to check with the nurse to make sure it's alright?" She asks.

I strip out of my shirt right there in front of her, hoping it will disarm her just enough. Possibly remind her how close we are. Make her think that it's wrong to keep anything from me.

"I don't have to do everything I tell Steve I'm going to," I offer with a wink.

But Cece doesn't smile back. She gives me a strange look. One that makes me think I've made a misstep. I quiet myself and finish undressing. She turns her back to me to do the same.

Silently, we climb onto our tables and cover ourselves, face down. I stare out the little hole in the headrest and try to come up with something intelligent to say when this is all over. Maybe the massage will relax her again. I wonder what I said wrong?

The two women come back into the room and I watch one of them pad over to a stereo by the wall. She pushes some buttons and some very Zen-inspiring music begins to play. It reminds me of the CDs you used to be able to sample at super centers in the 90s. And judging from the way it skips a couple of times on the first track, that might be where she got it from.

I'm almost tempted to just let myself enjoy the massage and allow my mind to clear. But I don't. Instead, my thoughts whir like little dust devils dancing through the desert, kicking up little bits of debris, only to get sucked up by another whirling thought.

If Cece saw something, why wouldn't she tell me?

She'd have to be afraid.

Afraid that Steve would be furious?

Possibly.

Afraid that I wouldn't believe her?

Also a possibility.

Too many women shoot the messenger when it comes

to matters of their relationships. I'd like to think I wouldn't do that. At this point, I'd be glad for the confirmation. At least then I wouldn't think I was nuts for continuing to circle back to the idea that my husband tried to off me last night.

Maybe Collin told her to stay out of it.

How could someone be that cold, though?

If you witnessed an attempted murder, wouldn't you say something?

We are in unusual circumstances. I remind myself.

Not only are we out of the country, but we're trapped on a boat together for the next several days. It's not like any of us can just get off and hike back to the airport. There's a literal jungle out there.

I need to be careful. I don't want to make her shut down entirely.

The thing I said about the Mahi Mahi helped. If only I could conjure a memory on command. Something that might help me make her feel closer to me.

It brings up the question again of how close we were to begin with.

If Cece were my best friend, she'd have told me already. I know that. We don't know each other as well as I'd hoped. Another point of proof for that is how she reacted to me teasing about not listening to Steve. Wouldn't a good friend call me out if they were upset?

And she had just gone cold.

I know she knows something, though.

After I'm commanded to roll over, the masseuse's fingers begin sliding up my neck and I grunt in pain.

"Ouch, sorry," I say. "Maybe not the neck."

"Of course," the woman says softly, as though she just forgot, even though I hadn't told her anything. It makes me wonder how much talking the crew has done behind the scenes.

I wonder if they've made the same comparison Helene did, pitting me against the woman that was eaten by the caiman.

The thought makes my nose wrinkle in disgust.

Sixty minutes after we undressed, the massage is over. The two women gently tell us we can take our time getting up and getting dressed.

I open my eyes slowly, and the pink lighting is over-whelming. Almost too bright now. Only a moment ago, it seemed dim. I take it in, inhaling deeply and telling myself I should enjoy it. I don't know how much relaxing I'll be able to do at any other point.

I roll my head to the side and stare over at Cece. She's still got her eyes closed, face turned straight at the ceiling.

"Are you in there?" I tease gently, my voice feeling far too loud even though it's only a whisper.

"That was wonderful," she admits.

She pulls herself upright and swings her legs over the side of the table, clutching her blanket to her chest. I roll over on my elbow to face her.

"It was lovely, wasn't it?" I say. Even as I say it, I know the massage stirred up some pain for me. My neck is aching again and I probably need a pain pill once we get out of here. I'm also aware of aches all over the rest of my body. The cost of falling off the second story of a riverboat, I suppose.

Cece gets up to get dressed, but I stay where I am.

She shrugs into her tank top.

"Cece?" I say her name.

"Hmm?" she doesn't turn around, only acknowledges me.

"We're good friends, aren't we?" I ask.

The question makes me sound vulnerable. I realize that. But it's occurred to me that I might have to give a little to get a lot.

She pauses right in the middle of pulling her tank top down. Frozen for a moment, the question has taken her off guard. Something I'd hoped it would do.

"Yes," she says, resuming her movement and letting the fabric settle around her waist. "Yes," she repeats, this time more firmly. "We are good friends."

She turns to face me.

"Why—why would you ask that?"

"I just—" I hesitate. There's a note in Cece's voice that puts the hairs on the back of my neck on end. I feel like an animal, its hackles standing up at an unseen threat it detects with its other senses. "Last night has me thinking. I just want you to know I appreciate you."

She stands there for a moment, blinking her only movement. Finally, she opens her mouth to speak, then closes it. She nods. "Thank you," she manages. There seems to be a lump in her throat.

I nod back at her.

And then Cece steps out into the hallway, leaving the door cracked to the unlit downstairs hallway.

Darkness pours in.

NINE

WHEN I EMERGE onto the main deck, the bright light pains my eyes. Maybe it's the head injury, but the ache seems to penetrate deep inside my skull. I need to go to the room and take a pain pill. For the moment, I do my best to look around the deck for my three companions, but I only find Steve.

Not shockingly, Cece and Collin seem to have retreated to their room.

I think about how weird she acted after the massage. How it was like I'd said something to upset her on purpose. I wave my arm broadly to catch Steve's eye. Finally, he notices and stands when he sees me, making his way across the back deck to where I'm at.

"I think I need a pain pill," I tell him.

He nods and leads the way to our room. He fishes the green motel-style diamond-shaped keychain out of his pocket and unlocks the door, allowing me to go in before him. I make a beeline for the bathroom and grab the pills out of my makeup bag, popping one into my mouth. I'm tempted to take another, but remind myself they're strong. Doubling up on opioids might not be the best course of action, given the state of things. No better than drinking too much, I would guess.

Maybe worse.

I tuck my hair behind my ears and look at myself in the mirror.

My face is bare and my skin is pasty, rather than sun-kissed. I need the vitamin D. My eyes are sunken and there are dark circles beneath them. Despite the fact that I slept last night, it was fitful. The whole time, all I kept thinking was that Steve would strangle me while I slept. It made it hard to get into anything other than a shallow, momentary loss of consciousness.

I take a deep breath and realize my hands are shaking.

Maybe it's the adrenaline of everything wearing off. Having a moment to myself in here. I step over to the door and close it behind me, acting like I'm going to use the toilet. Instead, I close the lid and sit down on top of it, trying to give myself a moment to think.

Everyone is acting strange.

What kind of secret are they all keeping?

I flush the toilet and return to the sink, washing my hands just for audio effect and because they could probably use it. Toweling them off, I reach for the bathroom door. I unlock it and grasp the doorknob, but my palm stills, lingering there for a moment. I steel myself before I have to go back into the room and be *on*.

"How was your massage?" Steve asks.

He is sitting on the edge of the bed as though he's just been waiting for me to come back out.

"It was great," I tell him. "Relaxing."

"I'm glad," he says. He pauses then, like he's thinking about saying something else. "I'm going to take a shower," he finally says.

Somehow, it's anticlimactic. I thought he might say something more exciting. Like *I know what you're thinking. Yes, I pushed you off the boat, you stupid whore.* Or *Tell me what you really remember, you bitch!*

Steve doesn't speak to me with those words, but I know he's thinking them.

There's a quiet rage radiating off of him. It has been since last night. Like I foiled all his plans by not just dying like I should have.

I want to tell him he should have covered his bases better. Maybe shot or strangled me. Strangling would have been the best. Quiet, concealable. He must have been mad.

He gets up and goes into the bathroom, quietly closing the door behind him.

I hear the lock click into place.

Why would he lock the door?

A little laugh escapes me. It's disbelief rather than finding any comic relief in the situation.

He knows I know.

He's making it harder for me to settle the score.

He *really* thinks I would kill him.

I laugh again, louder this time, and clap a hand over

my mouth. I hope he didn't hear me. I inhale sharply through my nose and tell myself to get a grip. Pacing back and forth, I bite my nails, and then I spot something.

Steve's cell phone.

He left it beside the bed.

What an idiot.

I rush over to the nightstand and grab his phone. Just as I'm about to put in the passcode, I glance at the door and realize it's still quiet in there. Finally, breathlessly, I wait for the sound of running water to start.

And it does.

I sigh in relief, my entire body relaxing as I do. I realize then how much tension I'm carrying, even after a massage. I type in the passcode. Four numbers. Our anniversary.

It's wrong.

The screen shakes back and forth, telling me that I've entered an incorrect passcode.

I try again, same passcode. Maybe I typed it in too quickly, reversed two of the numbers.

But it shakes again, telling me again that it's wrong.

Did he change his passcode?

It's been the same since we got married.

I used his phone to check the weather a week ago. The passcode was right then.

He's changed it in the last seven days.

I try his birthday. Wrong again.

I try his graduation year. Wrong yet again.

I'm warned that I have one more attempt.

My mind goes blank. What the hell could it be?

I try his mother's birthday and take a deep breath before hitting the last number.

It shakes again.

"Fuck!" I whisper.

The phone informs me it won't unlock again for an hour as a safety precaution.

Shit. Shit. Shit.

He'll know I was trying to get into it.

Blood thunders in my ears. The realization that I might be caught washes over me. I have to hide the phone. I take a deep breath, trying to calm myself down and slow my pulse so I can hear again. I strain my ears and the shower is still going. I breathe a sigh of relief for the second time.

I have a few minutes.

Glancing around the room, I look for a hiding spot. Somewhere I can put the phone that he won't find it. Somewhere that, when he does find it, it will seem logical that he might have put it there to begin with. Somewhere he won't think of for an hour.

My brain goes numb, unable to come up with anything. Everywhere I look seems too obvious.

I have to keep the phone on me. I have to hide it.

The shower shuts off.

I hear Steve getting out, and the towel rattles its holder on the wall.

I stand and power his phone off, then tuck it into the pocket of my pants. The white linen trousers are wide-leg and puffy. He won't see it there. I shut my own phone off and tuck it between the mattress and the box spring on my side of the bed. The last thing I want to do is grab my phone and make him think he needs his.

I need to distract him. Keep him from going straight to the nightstand.

Steve swings the door open and steps out into the room, just a towel wrapped around his waist. His prematurely white hair drips onto his chest and shoulders, and for a moment, I'm struck by how handsome he is. All the things about his physical appearance that made me notice him the first time.

I step around the bed and reach for him. He pulls me into an embrace and hugs me tightly. He smells my hair, something he's always done.

"God, I'm so glad you're alright," he says.

The way he says it, he's almost sad. And I remind myself that it could be that he truly *is sad* rather than anything nefarious. Is that wishful thinking on my part? I don't know. Not with the way he's holding me now.

He pulls away, the water from his hair on my skin now.

"I was afraid I was going to lose you," he says.

I swallow, nervous about what he might say next, though I can't really say why.

"And in that moment, when that's what it felt like was happening, all I could think of was when everything started."

I stand there silently. I know the memory well. Our first kiss.

"I thought maybe I was being punished," he admits

softly. "The whole thing just retribution for what I did to someone else."

The thought had occurred to me, too.

Punishment.

Divine judgment.

Both of us got off rather scot-free in that situation. For years, I worried that it would crop up at some point and ruin our lives. I guess, in that way, it's successfully haunted me. No shred of joy is protected from it. I can feel the shadow of what we did on all our brightest moments.

And right now, it almost feels biblical.

Why did I survive then?

Maybe my memory loss is my punishment. Having to live the rest of my life with a man I can't fully trust. A conclusion I should have come to just from the way our relationship started.

Maybe God really needed to make that apparent to me.

I'm fairly certain he hasn't left his Old Testament ways entirely behind.

"The thought crossed my mind," I admit quietly to my husband.

He touches my hair and smiles at me somewhat sadly.

"I guess it was bound to catch up with us," he says, a sad chuckle on his breath.

"I guess," I say.

Though I'm sure of it.

It was bound to catch up with us.
And in ways I never imagined.

TEN

STEVE TOUCHES MY FACE SOFTLY, tracing the line of my jaw. I always thought it was too strong, too masculine. But he cured me of that, spending hours tracing it with his finger and telling me how he'd never see a more perfect profile. That I looked like a statue carved by Michelangelo.

The sharp angles of my face never bothered Steve. Neither did my height.

It helps that he's several good inches taller.

I smile up at him, and he leans in, cradling my chin gently with his fingers. He kisses me, his mouth tasting clean and minty. Despite my situation, I find myself weak against his kiss. It's the same as it's always been. Like kryptonite to Superman.

Melting against him, my body responds. Even now, even when I think he could have tried to kill me, I want him. Our kisses are passionate, needful, growing ever more so by the second. He reaches for the hem of my shirt and snakes his palms up my back.

Two hot palms against my back.

I break from his kiss, gasping for air and feeling the room spin.

"You alright?" He's equally breathless. "Is it your head?"

"Just dizzy, that's all," I say.

"Here," he leads me to the bed and sits down, pulling me across his lap. He strokes my face again and I wrap my arms around his shoulders. I want so badly for everything to be back to the way it was. But the sensation of his hands against my skin sent me reeling.

It shot me right back to last night.

That was real.

"I don't want to hurt you," he says.

I pull away.

"What?" I ask, a nervous smile on my lips.

"Your head. I don't want to hurt you," he repeats.

I realize what he's talking about. Meaning he doesn't want to have sex if it's going to hurt me.

There's a part of me—a twisted, fucked up, unhinged part of me—that, beyond a shadow of a doubt, knows he tried to kill me last night. And that same part of me does not care.

I love Steve and I always have.

No one has ever made me feel the way he does.

And when he touches me, it reminds me of that all over again.

I cover his mouth with mine and he kisses me, spinning me around and laying me gently on my back. He undoes my bra with a flick of his wrist and pulls the garment out and tosses it onto the floor, all the while without breaking eye contact.

He reaches for the waist of my pants and then stops.

"Let me put this on the nightstand," he says.

I freeze.

The phone.

My heart races even faster. Sex and death collide in my mind and in my body.

He plucks the phone—identical to his—from my pocket and places it on my nightstand, unwittingly bedding me directly on top of my own.

Steve doesn't even give the phone a second glance. I sigh, relieved, though it sounds like desire, and he takes it as such. Maybe it is, partially.

He slides my pants off, throwing them on the floor and makes quick work of my underwear. His movements are primal, desperate. My own are just as needy. I wrap my legs around him as he positions himself, and then he thrusts into me.

His eyes roll back in his head and he groans my name.

"Fuck," he mutters.

He reaches down for me, pulling me up until I'm straddling him, completely upright. He moves slowly, being sure to fuck every inch of his cock into me. Like he's claiming me as his own for the first time all over again.

And I can't deny that it's intoxicating.

Any thought I had of escaping him is gone. I want to let this man destroy me however he sees fit. I would turn myself inside out for him. Go to the moon and back again. There's nothing I wouldn't sacrifice for Steve.

Including myself.

IT'S ONLY as we're lying in the afterglow that I realize I don't have a way of telling time without either of our phones.

I stare at the white ceiling, my mind racing and trying to think of ways to keep Steve from getting up, getting dressed, and searching for his iPhone. There's no way he won't want to check it soon. But right now, he's reminiscing about one of our first real dates. A time after we were both free. The first time we didn't have to sneak around.

I make the appropriate noises at the appropriate time, but after my orgasm the rose-tinted glasses I'd been looking at him with seem to have cleared a little. The man did try to kill me, after all. And right now, I need to keep him from turning on his phone for another fifteen minutes.

"I love you, Steph," he says.

"Hmm?" I ask, only halfway hearing his words.

"I said, 'I love you,'" he repeats. He looks at me.

"I love you, too," I say and press a kiss to his cheek.

I do love him.

But I'm afraid of him.

He starts to get up.

"No, stay," I say, staying firmly put with my head on his arm.

He leans back and laughs.

"We need to get ready for dinner soon," he says.

"That's not for a while," I tell him, though I don't know what time it is at all.

I curse myself for being so stupid. I should have gotten him out of the room.

"It's sooner than you think," he says. "Probably about an hour from now."

He tries to get up again and I feel like I have nothing to say to keep him lying down.

He stands and grabs his towel, carrying it back into the bathroom. I watch as he walks across the room naked to grab clothes from the closet. A white shirt and khaki shorts. Somehow, he'll manage to make the outfit look devastating. I know this about him.

When Steve walks into a room, he commands it.

I imagine it would be the same in an interrogation room if someone were to accuse him of attempted murder.

I'm not sure I have more to stand on here than a blurry memory. There's nothing else. I have no proof.

Steve grabs his clothes and heads back into the bathroom to get ready.

I go over to the closet, searching through my own clothes for something to wear.

I settle on a green maxi dress, but as I tug it from the rack, something catches my eye on top of my husband's suitcase.

Steve's shirt from last night.

A memory comes to me. The missing button.

I stare at the shirt, conjuring the memory to mind.

The top button is missing. Almost like the shirt was torn open.

Like Steve had been fighting with someone.

What if I had ripped the button off when we were arguing? What had we fought about? I struggle to bring it to mind. The hazy memories of recent weeks come back to me. Tension between us. Unrest in our home. It had felt nothing like it did today when we had sex.

That had felt like another time, deeply buried in the past.

Something is wrong in our marriage.

And I think Steve is willing to kill me over it.

ELEVEN

BY THE TIME STEVE CHANGES, the necessary remaining fifteen minutes have passed. I grab his phone on the nightstand and power it on while he freshens up in the bathroom.

I'm ready before Steve and I step out into the corridor. I walk down, out onto the very balcony from which I fell. I glance down at the wooden flooring, looking anywhere for his missing button, thinking that surely, at any moment, it's going to catch my eye and there will be my smoking gun.

Aha! You really did it!

And what then?

I step up to the railing, looking down at the river water below. There's a small dent on the edge of the deck. The place where I hit the fiberglass hull and went into the current. They've managed to clean any remaining blood from the site. Now it just looks like the boat hit the dock at a funny angle. Nothing so sinister as a passenger going overboard.

The boat advances down the river, leaving a gentle wake behind it. The scene is a far cry from last night. The sun is dropping in the sky, casting the river and jungle behind us in harsh late-in-the-day light. I imagine Golden Hour here is stunning. Not that I can remember it from the first two days of the trip.

"There you are," Steve says as he closes our door. He locks it with our key.

I turn from the railing and look back at him, offering a smile. Uneasiness makes me step to the side, crossing my arms over my chest. For some reason, I don't feel good about leaning on the railing just now.

He steps up to it and rests his hands on the polished wood, looking out at the jungle.

"Stunning, isn't it?" he asks.

I make a noise of affirmation, agreeing with him.

"You picked a lovely place for a vacation, Steph," he says, eyes still focused forward.

I don't tell him that if I had it to do over again, I'd pick somewhere less hazardous.

Despite the tension between us in the weeks leading up to the trip, I must not have foreseen the real danger I'd face once we left the United States.

Who would have?

No one.

You hear all the time about one spouse killing another. A woman goes overboard on a cruise to the Bahamas. A man encourages his wife to keep backing up until she backs up right over the edge of a cliff somewhere in Norway. It happens all the time, whether it makes the news or not.

But no one thinks it could happen to *them*.

Much like notions of all horrible things. They happen to others. Not to us.

"Are you having a good trip?" I ask him.

"All things considered," he says, turning to face me. "It's not too bad." He smiles. "Especially since you were alright after last night."

He reaches for my hand and I let him have it. He brings it to his lips, pressing a kiss like I'm some sort of royalty.

"I'm a bit glad of that myself," I tease.

For a moment, things feel solid. Like we're on even footing and like nothing bad happened. Like it really was all an accident. A thought comes to me that I know what I felt against my back. And unless I'm willing to surrender to the idea that my mind is against me, that really happened.

Could Steve not have done it?

There's a running joke with true crime fans that *the husband did it*.

There's a reason for that.

You are more statistically likely to be murdered by your significant other than anyone else in your life. And beyond them, it's likely to be someone you know. Stranger-on-stranger violence is rare, and we tend to gawk at it the most. Serial killers. Stalkers. Things like that catch our attention. Podcasts make more money when the stories are salacious rather than something that could happen in your own backyard. Something danger-ously ordinary.

I think it makes those stories all the more deadly.

It could happen to any one of us.

As though he's reading my mind, he says something that catches me off guard.

"I love you, Stephanie. I hope you know that."

The phrasing is what does it, sending the hair on the back of my neck upright with a tingle that tells me some-thing's wrong. I only nod, probably more vigorously than I need to. Suddenly, I feel vulnerable standing out here with him right at the spot where everything happened last night.

Surely to God he wouldn't go for a repeat.

I bark out a laugh unintentionally. The absurdity of my thoughts is catching up with me. A week ago, I was in a marriage just like any other, so far removed from those statistics. And now, I find myself right in the middle of a story that might end up on *Dateline*.

"I'm sorry," I say, turning instantly serious. "I think I'm still a little woozy from last night."

Steve furrows his brow, obviously hurt that I laughed at such an inopportune moment. I seize the chance to make it right.

"I love you so much," I tell him.

And it's not a lie, even though it's coated in pain now.

I don't know if there's any way back from this. If there's any path we can take from where we are to return to anything resembling normality. Not unless I can know for sure that he didn't shove me off this boat.

And I have a sinking feeling that he did.

Steve holds my hand, rubbing the back of it with his thumb, and I think I feel the way a moth feels when it stumbles into a spider's web.

Just then, Collin and Cece exit their room, right next door to ours.

I turn, startled, and jump a little. Steve drops my hand.

"Sorry we're late," Collin says with a pressed smile. Cece makes the same expression.

I force a smile at both of them, getting the distinct impression that they've been fighting. I didn't hear anything coming from their room next to ours. I imagine them whispering back and forth; him grabbing her wrist, her jerking away.

It's a wild assumption. They probably weren't fighting at all.

"No, no, you're fine," I say.

Collin's smile warms slightly.

"Shall we?" Steve asks, gesturing toward the little twisting staircase that we have to take one at a time in order to fit.

Downstairs, other couples and groups are seated at their respective tables and we make our way to ours. I let Steve lead the way, assuming we're headed for the only empty one near the front of the boat, but not certain.

I take the seat nearest the water and Collin sits directly across from me. Cece and Steve take their seats and everyone indulges in small talk after we put in our drink orders. I only ask for water, once again thinking that mixing alcohol with the pain pills might be a bad idea.

After a moment, everyone falls silent. The talk slowly dies, and I'm left with the unshakable feeling that there's some unspoken tension between everyone. I try to think of something to break it, as it becomes almost unbearable.

"Lovely views," I say. Everyone looks at me. Cece smiles and nods. Collin gives me a halfhearted grin, and Steve stares into his whiskey on the rocks. I clear my throat and take a drink of water.

Above the rainforest, the sun is beginning to set, and I was right. Golden Hour spent sailing down the Amazon River is a sight to behold. For a moment, I'm sucked into its beauty, forgetting my own troubles. But it's brief, and the clatter of a knife dropping out of a rolled napkin brings me back to reality.

"Cece tells me that the two of you enjoyed your massage," Collin says with a smile that has to be false, stretched so tightly over his features he looks like he might explode into a million pieces.

"It was great," I say. "Wasn't it?" I ask Cece.

"Oh, yeah. Fantastic," she says halfheartedly.

Her mind is elsewhere. I feel my brow furrow and fight the expression.

Collin clears his throat.

"I'll be right back," Steve says, standing from the table and excusing himself. I crane my neck around to watch him leave the dining area. Just as I turn around, preparing to make some lighthearted remark, Cece gets up from the table as well.

"Not a bad idea. I think I need to use the restroom," she says, and walks quickly out of sight toward the downstairs bathroom.

I turn and face Collin.

"Am I that off-putting?" I tease.

But Collin gives me a nervous laugh and a smile that's even more uneasy.

"What?" I ask.

There's a part of me that just wants to demand they tell me what's going on. There's another part of me that realizes the danger here is very real. I search Collin's face.

"Nothing," he says brightly, sipping his mixed drink. He sets it down and looks at me again, this time with a seriousness on his face. "How are you doing, Steph?" he asks.

It's the nickname that catches me off guard.

"Fine," I say with a smile.

"No, really," he says. He leans forward across the table and I find myself leaning back into my seat in response to his intensity.

"I—" I struggle for the right thing to say, unsure of what he wants from me. "I'm fine. Really."

He reaches for me across the table, grabbing my wrist hard. Hard enough that I'm afraid it will leave a bruise.

"Ouch," I say. "You're hurting me." I smile at him, though I feel the prick of tears in my eyes.

"You don't remember anything, do you?"

He looks as though he's going to come across the table and wrap both hands around my neck. I'm taken aback by the confrontation. And just like that, he lets go of me, falling back into his relaxed position across the table. I stare at him, blinking rapidly.

"Much better," Steve says and I swipe at the tear that almost spilled. Cece is standing next to him.

I turn, facing my husband. The shock of Collin's pointed question hasn't worn off as Steve sits down. I compose myself, though, and continue as though nothing strange has happened.

"Good," I say brightly, looking at him. I glance at Collin, but he's looking at Steve, too. Smiling at him, even. As though he didn't just threaten me.

Steve takes his glass in hand and speaks.

"I know the last twenty-four hours have been quite shocking, to say the least," he says with a dark chuckle. "But I wanted to raise a toast. To us."

The three of us seem shocked into stillness. The awkwardness from moments ago has returned, amplified by Steve's proposed celebration.

What's going on?

"To us," he repeats, raising his glass of whiskey.

Cece follows suit and so do I, touching our glasses in the center of the table. Finally, Collin joins us. "To us," we all chorus.

The glasses clink together, a sound that usually indicates happier times. Maybe that's what Steve was going for. My eyes flit over to Collin and I find him staring at me. I look away quickly, feeling self-conscious and suddenly not wanting to be anywhere he is.

I take a sip of my water and smile at my companions.

You don't remember anything, do you?

The question echoes in my mind throughout our meal.

Maybe it's best if I don't.

But something isn't right.

At the end of the dinner, the sun has set, and darkness has returned to our boat. Dim ambient lights hang romantically along the railing above us, illuminating our seating arrangement daintily.

I glance at Steve and catch him looking at me.

There's love in his eyes. Adoration. Gratitude.

Maybe he's grateful he didn't kill me. Maybe things are looking up.

I smile and look away, accidentally glancing across the table at Collin, his arm around his wife, a frown on his face.

Or maybe it wasn't Steve that had it out for me after all.

TWELVE

THE CROWD *we ran with loved dinner parties. Around any holiday, that's all we did. Fourth of July meant an explosive, all-night pool party at our house in the Hills. Halloween meant costume balls in obscenely large homes with rented dance floors for the night. Christmas brought the true dinner parties. Intimate gatherings with red wine and heartier fare.*

But throughout that holiday season, there was one constant.

You.

And our budding affair.

He never really cared what I did during our parties, so long as I showed our guests a good time and made him look like a winner with me on his arm at the appropriate moments. Hellos, goodbyes, toasts.

But we shared so many secret moments. From July, all the way through New Year's Eve.

I remember sparklers in our hands, out by the pool.

We'd run into each other during the party, both of us without our better half. You stopped and stared at me, mouth slightly open, with a grin on your face. The shimmering sparks bounced off the pool and lit your face from beneath, casting dancing shadows across your features.

We fucked beside the house that night, all the while the party raged on.

We could have been caught. It was half the fun.

You stole a kiss before you slunk back in, looking for your wife.

I went to the bathroom and wiped my lipstick off, making sure there was no evidence it had worn off by any other means than drinking my champagne all night. He never suspected anything.

It went on like that, all through the fall. All through the holidays. And then New Year's Eve was upon us.

You insisted that we share a kiss at midnight.

We had to coordinate it just right, both of us sneaking away just before the clock struck twelve. I met you in the hallway between the game room and the living room. The lights were out. Everyone was counting down from ten, following along with someone's watch, poised to blow their noisemakers at just the right second.

You smiled at me devilishly, but then it faltered.

There was something vulnerable about it. Something that I hadn't seen from you before, at least not this clearly. In that moment, I felt like I could see your soul. I knew exactly how you felt about us.

"Happy New Year!" The party shouted from the other room, and you crushed your mouth against mine. The kiss

was different, needful in a way I wasn't expecting. You pulled away.

"I love you, Stephanie," you whispered. "I've been in love with you for a long time."

I felt breathless, my heart thundering in my chest like it hadn't since my first kiss.

It was the first time you told me you loved me, and the moment I realized that this was something beyond just a physical affair. I'd had feelings for you, but I'd been afraid I was being naïve.

It turned out we'd felt the same.

What we were doing no longer felt dirty.

It felt important. Like we were moving toward something bigger. A better future than either of us could have imagined at the time. It gave meaning to our little trysts and rendezvous. And it made me realize how unhappy I really was.

You were a way out.

Realizing that this was more than a physical affair let me be honest with myself. I'd been in love with you since I met you. And I hadn't felt that way in so long.

I knew then that we were set on a collision course with fate.

That one day I'd be your wife.

That one day we'd be able to have our own life, away from all the things that made us unhappy.

And in that moment, I knew that was all I wanted.

Just you and our future.

THIRTEEN

WHEN I CRAWL into bed that night, I'm left obsessing about the way that Collin looked at me.

Like a madman, ready to reach across the table and shake me.

It's so disconcerting that the fact that I'm sleeping with my back pressed against Steve's doesn't even bother me. Suddenly, he feels non-threatening, and I'd be happy to spend the rest of the trip hiding in the room with him.

But I can hardly tell him that.

I wonder if he realizes I don't remember them. Surely, at some moment, it will occur to him. Something will ring false, or maybe he'll have a premonition. Some innate knowing might come over him. The thought fills me with dread.

I listen to Steve's breathing. He snores lightly, falling asleep as easily as if nothing were out of sorts.

Should he be able to sleep that easily?

Would I sleep that easily if he had gone overboard? Not if I thought he'd been pushed.

If I was worried that someone had pushed him, I wouldn't be able to sleep. And I'd have already said something to him about it.

Unless *I* was the one who pushed him.

Or knew who was.

Steve is sleeping like a man who has nothing to worry about.

I roll over and stare at him, watching the side of his ribcage rise and fall with his snores. I try to reconcile the man I've known all these years with someone who might have pushed me overboard.

There's no way he did it.

None of it adds up.

But when I think about Collin staring at me from across the table tonight, my wrist in his hand, it makes my anxieties take a different direction.

Steve's phone begins to vibrate on the nightstand, startling me and making me jump. I sit up in bed and look over at it.

A number I don't recognize, local to Los Angeles, is calling.

Without thinking, I reach across my husband and grab the phone. I pick it up and swipe, then hold it to my ear, holding my breath.

"Mr. Silkwood?" A man's voice on the other end comes through just as clearly as if we were across town from him right now.

I glance at Steve, snoozing peacefully.

"Hello?"

"Hello," I whisper.

The man on the other end of the phone pauses for a moment, obviously not expecting anyone but Steve to answer.

"Who is this?" I ask.

"Mr. Silkwood?" the man asks, less confidently this time.

"I'm his assistant," I say softly. "He's uh—out of town just now and had his calls forwarded. What can I help you with?"

"I'm calling from Smith and Turner about the paper-work that Mr. Silkwood requested last week. Is it alright that I send it to the fax at his office?"

"That's fine," I say. "I'll be on the lookout for it."

"Great. I hope Mr. Silkwood enjoys his vacation," the man says, and then hangs up.

I stare at the phone for a moment, then lock it and place it on the nightstand next to Steve.

The name sounds familiar. I could swear I've heard it on a commercial or maybe seen it on a billboard. Not the kind of lawyer that Steve normally deals with. No, the lawyers he employs don't advertise.

I grab my phone, and curiosity gets the best of me.

I type in the name into the search engine, followed by *Los Angeles*. But before I hit enter, I hear something. I look up, straining my ears to see if I just imagined it.

An argument next door. It's coming from Collin and Cece's room.

I lock my phone and stand up, trying not to make the

bed creak as I do so. I step quietly into the bathroom and grab the glass sitting unused on the sink. I step into the shower. It's the closest to the wall that separates us. I cringe as the glass clinks against the tile of the shower, then I press my ear to it, and I listen.

"—fucked it all up!" Cece says. I only catch the tail-end of what sounds like an accusation.

"You're insane, you know that, right?" Collin asks, his tone even though on the verge of angry.

"*I'm* insane?" Cece says, her voice climbing an octave with the question.

"Don't ruin this trip," Collin says.

"Ruin the trip?" She laughs. "I think you've already managed that."

She stomps away to the other side of the room. I press the glass harder against the tile, and in a split second, it slips and tumbles to the bottom of the shower, shattering.

"Steph?" I hear Steve in the other room. My heart thuds.

I step out of the shower and stand there in the bath-room for a moment, gathering my thoughts. Before I can, he's at the doorway, sleepy-eyed but looking concerned.

"I slipped," I blurt. "I got a drink of water and spilled some on the floor and slipped. It broke in the shower."

The words come out in a rush, like I'm a child confessing to having stolen something my father told me I couldn't have. Steve walks over to me and rubs my tight shoulders. He looks at me in the mirror, only the moon-light reflecting off the river illuminating his handsome face.

"You've been through a lot," he says.

I only nod, thinking that had he been a moment sooner, he would have realized I was eavesdropping on our friends. Swallowing, I feel the lump in my throat bob up and down. I wonder if Steve notices it, but he doesn't seem to.

"Let's go back to bed. I'll get that taken care of in the morning. Is it all in the shower?"

I nod, making an affirmative sound.

"Let's go to bed," he repeats, and steps out from behind me, then gently tugs me that way.

I follow him and climb back into bed. I pull the covers up around my chin. Steve scoots closer, his back touching my arm as I lie there. Almost instantly, he's asleep again.

I stare at the ceiling.

Ruin the trip? I think you've already managed that.

I hear Cece's laugh. A barking sound, hardly pleasant and definitely not full of joy. Combining her statement with the way Collin looked at me, and what he said, alarm bells start to go off inside my head.

She knows.

He's the one who pushed me.

I'm certain of it.

I roll over and face the wall on my side of the bed. My phone lights up on the nightstand, a notification. Thank God the boat has satellite internet. We paid extra for that.

It's just Instagram, but I pick the phone up anyway. I unlock it and stare at the screen. My search terms are sitting there. I hit search and the results populate slowly.

The first one catches my eye, and I stare at it for a long time.

Smith and Turner Los Angeles - Divorce Attorneys

I struggle to process what I'm seeing, wondering if there's been a mistake.

Why would Steve be contacting a divorce attorney?

I tap the link, going to their website. I read their bios and comb through the available pictures that paint them as the consummately professional law office.

My husband wanted paperwork from a divorce attorney.

And I had no idea.

I lock my phone and lie there in the dark as he snores next to me.

I think about how he just told me how much he loves me. How relieved he was that I'm okay. The sex, better than it had been in a long time. I felt connected to him in a way I'd missed somehow in the day-to-day normalcy of our lives.

We'd gotten complacent. Too comfortable.

That initial spark. The excitement of sneaking around had cooled.

Maybe Steve is done. Maybe he was waiting to spring it on me when we get back home.

I can't wait that long.

I'm going to confront him about it.

Tomorrow.

FOURTEEN

THE BOAT DOCKS at a scheduled stop the next day. It's an excursion that we signed up for when we booked the trip, but going deep into the jungle is the least of my worries. I don't sleep at all and I don't take my pain pills in the morning. I want to be fully with it when I talk to Steve.

I watch him get ready, changing into the hiking gear he so carefully picked out last month. I remember the outing. Such a normal day. One that I took for granted. It occurs to me how bland our life had become versus how it started. Maybe I'm not able to sustain the level of excitement that Steve wants.

Sitting there on the bed watching him, I lose track of time and almost make us late. He fusses at me finally, telling me to hurry up gently. There's an affection in his voice.

I wonder if that affection wouldn't be there if he really planned on divorcing me.

I have to talk to him.

Taking a moment to myself, I change in the bathroom and look at myself in the mirror in hopes of giving myself a pep talk. Instead, I only notice how tired I look. The bags under my eyes have only gotten worse and there's no point in wearing makeup today. This is as good as it gets. Somehow, I feel like I need to look prettier if I'm going to beg for my marriage.

"Are you ready?" Steve calls from the other room.

I hurry out and smile at him. He smiles in return.

"You look good," he says.

"Are you planning to divorce me?" I ask.

The words come out in a rush. I don't mean to ask it now. I meant to wait for the best possible moment, but I can't wait any longer. I need to know what's happening.

Steve stands there, his smile falters, replaced by something more serious, and he's quiet for a moment.

It gives me a sinking feeling in my gut.

"No," he says finally. "Why would you think that?"

"You got a call last night," I say. "You were already asleep, and it was a Los Angeles number. I answered. They wanted to send you paperwork. I looked up the name of the firm and they're divorce attorneys."

I say it all as matter-of-fact as I can, hoping that he can't detect the emotion in my voice. It threatens to break. I don't know if I can handle almost dying and finding out I'm getting divorced in the same week, but I'm sure there are people who've survived worse.

It feels like an eternity before he says something.

"That?" He laughs. "That wasn't for me."

My brow furrows. I stare at him, confused.

"Don't say anything," he says softly, glancing toward the wall we share with Collin and Cece. "But I called for Collin. He didn't want Cece to see the papers or be able to see who he had been talking to. It has nothing to do with us," he says with an easygoing smile.

"They're getting divorced?" I ask.

Though I don't remember anything about their relationship, it still comes as a shock. I guess divorce always does when it's people you know.

"I don't know. Look, don't say anything to her," he says. "I wasn't even going to tell you because I know that the two of you get to talking when you drink."

I stare at him blankly. Trying to reconcile the hostile version of Cece that I've come to know in the last day and a half with a woman that I might share secrets with over a glass of chardonnay.

"I won't," I assure him.

He gives me a grateful look. But then it's replaced with something else.

"Speaking of the two of you, you haven't really spent much time talking since the other night," he says.

I'm no detective, but I feel like Steve is sussing something out.

"Well, we haven't really had any time," I offer.

"You had that massage," he says.

"There wasn't much time for talking. We were both relaxing," I say, trying to sound nonchalant.

He looks at me and I'm sure he's suspicious. I flinch

under his gaze, wishing he'd break it, look away, and give it a rest.

"It's just unlike the two of you," Steve says.

"Well," I say. "Shall we?"

I gesture toward the door and indicate it's time to leave.

The relief I felt only moments ago is replaced with a suspicion that my husband knows something is up with me. Should I tell him?

I wonder if I had any idea about the divorce before the trip. What if I said something to Cece already? What if that's why they're fighting?

What if that's why Collin pushed me?

I got a little too involved in someone else's marriage. It's something I could see myself doing, especially for someone I considered a friend. Maybe Cece is in the process of shooting the messenger. Maybe she's mad at me for telling her.

Steve steps out into the hallway after me and locks the door.

We head down to the dock and Collin and Cece are waiting for us, ready to hike off into the jungle. There are two other couples joining us. One of them seems to be from Australia, judging from their accents. The other couple sounds German.

Collin and Cece greet us, but say little else. I think about the fight I overheard, and I wonder if it had to do with their impending divorce. How awkward if Cece found out on the trip. She told him he'd already ruined it. Maybe she meant by looking for a divorce.

I keep my distance from Collin. Our guide arrives, and I'm surprised to find that he's an American named Tyler who has left civilization behind to study the wildlife of the rainforest. I guess I was expecting a local.

Tyler's hair is long, pulled back into a ponytail at the base of his neck. His smile is genuine and broad, revealing two rows of big, imperfect teeth that are startlingly white.

"One thing before we head out," Tyler says after going over some basic safety with us. "Don't separate from the group. If you think getting lost at Disney World is bad, you really don't want to get lost out here. You could be ten feet off the trail and we'd never find you."

The thought is chilling.

"And in the highly unlikely event that you see a jungle cat, make yourself as big as possible, don't make any sudden movements, and above all else, do *not* turn your back on it."

The final warning reminds me that we really are in the middle of nowhere. The riverboat might be full of rich tourists, but out here in the jungle, money can't buy your safety. The best it can do is get you a guy like Tyler who gives half-hearted advice about what to do if you cross paths with a jaguar.

It strikes me how dangerous this might be, and I step closer to Steve until our arms touch. He looks over at me and smiles, seemingly unfazed by Tyler's warnings.

And without much more fanfare, Tyler sets off from the dock into the jungle in front of us.

Cece goes first and Collin follows her. Steve takes his

spot behind Collin, and I do my best to put the most distance I can between myself and Collin. The last thing I want is to be out in the jungle with him if he decides to get mad at me again.

Behind me is the German couple and ahead of Cece are the Australians.

Tyler speaks loudly so that we can all hear him and tells us about how he lives nearby at a remote research center and that he and another biologist actually cut the trail that we're using. He makes money taking tourists through the jungle because, as it turns out, you probably won't get rich studying Capuchin monkeys in the Amazon, and Tyler likes to fly home to Oklahoma from time to time.

I find myself tuning him out somewhere after that. I focus on the trail, putting one foot in front of the other and looking for snakes. Another piece of his advice. The thought occurs to me that if a snake bit me out here, I'd probably die, even though Tyler didn't confirm that. Any hospital is too long a distance away. I can't imagine how anyone would survive a truly deadly bite.

Maybe it's the head injury, but I begin to slow down and the distance between Steve and myself increases on the trail. Tyler's voice becomes muted by the dense foliage. The German couple picks up the pace and passes me. That's when I realize that I've really slowed down.

I glance up the trail and see the German couple disappearing around a tree. Struggling to pick up the pace, I begin to hear myself growing short of breath.

Christ. That fall really took it out of you.

I push onward, telling myself I need to catch up to the group. I'm far too far behind them now. I can't even hear Tyler. Forcing myself to calm down, I just put one foot in front of the other and focus all my attention on the trail beneath me. The trail will lead me to them. It's the one instruction Tyler gave if anyone were to fall behind.

Just don't leave the trail.

I keep pushing, and my calves begin to ache. Hiking isn't my forte and I can't remember the last time Steve and I did anything remotely this athletic. Bending at the waist, I try to catch my breath and stretch my legs.

That's when I hear it.

The cracking of a branch.

Snap!

Instinctively, I freeze. In that moment, it washes over me that I'm alone in the jungle. We've been hiking for a good thirty minutes. I have no idea where I'm at, only that I need to follow the trail one of two ways to get out of this jungle. And I just heard someone or something step on a stick.

I swallow, feeling my throat grow tight as I do so. Standing upright, I realize my mouth is dry. I don't dare take a drink of water and I'm overcome by the distinct sensation that I'm being watched.

I feel eyes on me, and the jungle goes eerily quiet.

I might be from Los Angeles, but I've seen enough nature documentaries to know that's not good.

It's the sign of a large predator.

I force myself to slow down my breathing, and I become very still. Slowly, I spin around.

And like a magnet is leading me, I lock eyes with it, crouched on the large branch of a tree, ready to leap at the slightest provocation.

It's a jaguar.

Silent as the night, it snuck up on me just like that.

The cat's tail flicks back and forth, eerily similar to a house cat having found a mouse.

I want to scream. For a moment, my mind goes blank, but suddenly Tyler's advice comes to me.

Make yourself as big as possible, no sudden movements, and do not turn your back on it.

I hear my breathing grow shallow as my heart picks up the pace. On the verge of having an out-of-body experience, the cat moves and I snap back to reality and the knowledge that this is most certainly *really* happening.

It stands up slightly, almost like it's thinking about jumping down from the tree.

"Steph!" Steve's voice calls down the trail.

I stretch my arms outward and puff up my chest. I stare at the cat, not breaking eye contact. I make myself as big as possible. I stand tall and stare at it.

The cat seems to size me up, wondering if it's worth it. If *I'm* worth it.

She's thinking about eating you.

God, what I would give for her to be one of Tyler's precious monkeys. Monkeys are mean, but I think I could fight off a Capuchin. I can't fight off a jaguar. Not without a powerful weapon, and I have nothing.

"Stephanie!" Steve calls again.

"I'm here!" I shout, hoping that the sudden sound

might startle the cat rather than trigger an attack, but it sits there and tilts its head slightly, tail still flicking back and forth in curiosity.

The jaguar isn't afraid of me. It's not afraid of the noises I make.

I hear footfalls coming through the jungle and I catch something yellow out of the corner of my eye. A shirt.

The cat whips its head around at the sound of someone else joining us.

And just like that, it hops from its perch and runs right past me.

I spin, my eyes following it, hardly believing that it just brushed me on its way elsewhere. I'm left breathless, with the distinct feeling that I've had a supernatural experience merely by being in its presence and living to tell the tale.

"Fuck," Collin mutters behind me.

I turn to face him, an involuntary smile splitting across my face as I let out a hysterical laugh.

He swallows, realizing the gravity of the situation, but he doesn't laugh. I turn back to the direction where the cat ran off but see no sign of her.

"It could have killed you," he says softly, almost under his breath.

I turn back to him, my trepidation about being alone with him replaced with relief that anyone at all has come to my rescue.

I walk his way, glancing twice behind me as I close the distance between Collin and me.

It's only when I'm next to him that the reality of

being alone with him begins to sink in. I step backwards, increasing the distance between us. Suddenly, I'm wishing the cat was still here instead.

"Are you alright?" Collin asks.

There's a true note of concern in his voice. A warmth to it.

He reaches out and squeezes my shoulders. I nod at him, wordless. He nods in return.

"I was afraid you'd gotten lost."

"We should get back to everyone," I say. "I bet they're waiting on us."

Collin's grip on my shoulders intensifies.

"What do you remember about the other night, Stephanie?"

His gaze implores me to answer. His grip grows firmer with every second I don't answer. I shake my head, unsure of what to say.

"I don't remember anything," I say, trying to reassure him that his secret is safe with me. I shake my head as I say it, a franticness to get away from him growing inside me.

"Did he hurt you?" he asks.

I stare at him, my shaking head beginning to still.

"Who?" I ask, completely clueless.

"Steve!" he says.

"What?" The question comes out as a breath. I don't know what he's talking about. He's got that same crazed look in his eye. "I'm sorry about you and Cece," I say. "If I told her, I didn't mean to." It comes rushing out of me, a confession. Anything to get him to let me go.

much as we can take. You're both risking the ruination of your respective lives for stolen moments with one another. It's heady stuff.

And I was fully under its sway.

Your phone began to buzz in your pocket, shattering any remaining notion that the moment was sacred or belonged to us at all. When you pulled it from your pocket, you frowned.

"I have to take this," you said. "I'm sorry."

I knew it was her. Likely calling to ask you to pick up dinner on your way home. A routine request that made me burn with jealousy. I could have your truant afternoons at the zoo, but not your mundane evenings with Chinese takeout in front of the television.

I longed for that.

When you got off the phone, you hugged me once again.

"We've got about fifteen minutes," you said.

Ah, there it was. The timer. She always put a timer on us. When she beckoned, you came. And it made me insanely jealous. How could you claim to be in love with me and still answer to her?

Saying I love you *had made things complicated.*

We kissed goodbye in the parking lot, and I sat in my SUV for an hour after you left. I listened to an album you'd told me was your favorite. I'd been surprised. Lana Del Ray. Not something I'd heard from a man before. But her songs seemed to fit our situation. Doomed love.

I didn't want to go home yet. As long as I stayed in the parking lot, I was still yours.

The moment I walked in the door at home, I was his.

I thought right then about leaving you both. Just running away to Las Vegas. Assuming a name and starting over. I could go back to dancing. I was skilled enough, and even though I was older, I was still fit and beautiful. I wouldn't be living the lifestyle I was in that moment, but I'd be able to take care of myself comfortably.

And I could start over.

Without any men telling me what to do or what they wanted me to be.

No men. The idea was as intoxicating as our affair had been in the beginning.

I'd had a friend in high school who told me I was demented because once I'd told her there was nothing quite as energizing as the end of a relationship.

"How could you say that?" she'd asked, giggling in shock at what I'd said. She was dating the quarterback. They went on to get married and have two and a half kids and a white picket fence.

"Freedom," I'd said. "It's the closest that a woman ever gets to being truly free. In those first minutes after you break his heart, anything is possible."

She'd stared at me like she was half afraid and half in awe.

The idea of leaving L.A. and leaving both of you was tempting.

That would have been freedom.

But just then, my phone rang. I answered it with my car stereo, cutting Lana off mid-sentence.

"Yeah," I said.

"Tell her what?" he asks.

"That you're divorcing her," I say.

He stares at me, puzzled. His gaze intense, he searches my face for any other clue. I don't know what to give him.

"What are you talking about?" he asks, furrowing his brow.

"There you are!" Steve's voice booms against the canopy of trees. Collin turns to face him, his hands falling from my shoulders. I'm so grateful I could cry. I run to embrace Steve and I jump onto him, wrapping my legs around his waist.

"I saw a fucking jaguar." I sob, not realizing I'm crying until the words rip from my throat.

"Holy shit," Steve says. "Are you alright?" He pulls back and I put my feet back onto the ground. The rest of the group starts coming down the trail in the distance.

"I'm fine," I tell him.

He looks me over, examining me for any evidence that I might not be.

"I never should have left you," he says.

I glance over at Collin. He just stands there, staring at us.

Finally, he steps past us, joining Cece on the trail. She says nothing when he reaches her, but she stares at me and Steve.

"It's okay," I tell him. "I just wasn't as prepared as I thought I was for this."

Starting to calm down, I swipe at the tears on my face and wipe my nose with the hem of my shirt.

"Do you want to go back to the boat?" he asks.

I glance at Collin, who hasn't broken his gaze from us.

"I think so," I say with a nod.

"That's fine," Steve assures me.

"It's better that we all stay together," Tyler says from behind us.

"We can go on," I tell Steve. "It's okay."

"I won't leave you," he says, squeezing me into another embrace.

When I open my eyes with my chin on his shoulder, I lock eyes with Collin, his stare blank.

FIFTEEN

THERE WAS *a jaguar at the Los Angeles Zoo. As we stood in front of it, you told me that zoos have a* kill-on-sight *list in the event that any or all of the animals should get out. The jaguar is on the list, you'd said.*

"Why?" I asked. "It's too beautiful to be on a list like that."

"A lot of beautiful things can kill you," you said with a smirk.

"Like me?" I asked.

You placed a kiss on my cheek and pulled me closer. The jaguar went back inside its indoor enclosure, where it was warmer. There was hardly anyone at the zoo. It was January and most of the animals were just trying to keep warm. It was the perfect place to go on a date with the man I was having an affair with.

I shivered. It was a cold day for L.A. and I was wearing a sweater. You pulled me closer.

"Maybe next time we'll go to the Tar Pits."

"That would be nice," I said.

But there was a sad note to it.

We were still sneaking around. It had only been a few weeks since you'd told me you loved me. I was still making room in my head for the idea that this could turn into something real. Something real enough to upend both our lives.

I wanted to be able to go somewhere with you and not worry about who might see us.

I wanted you to take me to dinner at my favorite restaurant.

But I knew that wasn't going to happen. At least not yet.

Realizing we were in love had been a revelation, and planning the exits for both of our marriages would be an affair entirely of its own.

"It won't be long," you whispered, as though you'd read my mind.

We'd been in sync like that for a while. You finished my sentences, my thoughts. In that moment, I wondered if I could ever be mad at you for any length of time.

The way you hugged me, even then, was exactly what I needed. You were so tall and strong, and when you squeezed me up against you, I felt like everything was right in the world. If the jaguar had jumped out of its enclosure, it's your embrace I would have sought.

We could survive anything, I realized.

Affairs create that illusion. Sharing a devastating secret can bond two people unlike anything else. But at the end of the day, we're both human and we can take only as

much as we can take. You're both risking the ruination of your respective lives for stolen moments with one another. It's heady stuff.

And I was fully under its sway.

Your phone began to buzz in your pocket, shattering any remaining notion that the moment was sacred or belonged to us at all. When you pulled it from your pocket, you frowned.

"I have to take this," you said. "I'm sorry."

I knew it was her. Likely calling to ask you to pick up dinner on your way home. A routine request that made me burn with jealousy. I could have your truant afternoons at the zoo, but not your mundane evenings with Chinese takeout in front of the television.

I longed for that.

When you got off the phone, you hugged me once again.

"We've got about fifteen minutes," you said.

Ah, there it was. The timer. She always put a timer on us. When she beckoned, you came. And it made me insanely jealous. How could you claim to be in love with me and still answer to her?

Saying I love you *had made things complicated.*

We kissed goodbye in the parking lot, and I sat in my SUV for an hour after you left. I listened to an album you'd told me was your favorite. I'd been surprised. Lana Del Ray. Not something I'd heard from a man before. But her songs seemed to fit our situation. Doomed love.

I didn't want to go home yet. As long as I stayed in the parking lot, I was still yours.

The moment I walked in the door at home, I was his.

I thought right then about leaving you both. Just running away to Las Vegas. Assuming a name and starting over. I could go back to dancing. I was skilled enough, and even though I was older, I was still fit and beautiful. I wouldn't be living the lifestyle I was in that moment, but I'd be able to take care of myself comfortably.

And I could start over.

Without any men telling me what to do or what they wanted me to be.

No men. The idea was as intoxicating as our affair had been in the beginning.

I'd had a friend in high school who told me I was demented because once I'd told her there was nothing quite as energizing as the end of a relationship.

"How could you say that?" she'd asked, giggling in shock at what I'd said. She was dating the quarterback. They went on to get married and have two and a half kids and a white picket fence.

"Freedom," I'd said. "It's the closest that a woman ever gets to being truly free. In those first minutes after you break his heart, anything is possible."

She'd stared at me like she was half afraid and half in awe.

The idea of leaving L.A. and leaving both of you was tempting.

That would have been freedom.

But just then, my phone rang. I answered it with my car stereo, cutting Lana off mid-sentence.

"Yeah," I said.

"Everything alright?" he asked.

I'd told him I'd been meeting a girlfriend for dinner. I glanced at the clock. It was later than I'd meant to stay out.

"I'm on my way home now. Just left the restaurant," I said.

"How was Vanessa?" he asked.

"She's good," I said. *"Really good. Freshly out of a relationship and starting fresh. Lucky girl, if you ask me,"* I half-teased.

And he laughed like that idea of lucky was the most absurd thing he'd ever heard.

SIXTEEN

BACK ON THE BOAT, standing under the showerhead, I let the hottest water I can get scald my skin until it's beet red. And then I flip the faucet to cold, one of my simplest pleasures.

It's something I do at home all the time. Take a hot shower—as hot as I can stand—and then turn it cold, as cold as it will go—and stand there, the sensation making me gasp like I've almost just drowned.

I gasp now as icy little streams of water run down my body. I let the water penetrate to my scalp and feel the strange way it plays with the stitches there. The spot is almost too sensitive, and I step out from under the direct flow of the water for a moment.

The whole time I've been showering, I've been thinking about the jaguar.

Within one week, I've come closer to dying—*twice*—than I ever have before in my entire life.

The jaguar's eyes are burned into my brain. So bright

and curious. So aware. Looking at them, you could see the gears in its mind turning. You knew exactly what it was thinking. It was like it was human, almost.

It had been one of the strangest, most surreal experiences of my life.

When I kill the water, I stand there, dripping for a minute or two. I realize that I almost wasn't able to take another hot and cold shower. I could have died out there today.

It's a fact that Steve is entirely too conscious of.

Almost losing me once was one thing, but now he's hovering like letting me out of his sight will spell the end of me. He even made me leave the door open while I showered.

"You alright?" he calls from the other room.

"I'm fine," I say, my voice coming out more listless and monotone than I mean for it to. Shouldn't I be filled with a zest for life right now? Shouldn't everything burn a little brighter?

Maybe it was the intensity of the experience today, but somehow everything seems dulled.

Or maybe it's the fact that my head has started to hurt as the day has worn on. I need a pain pill.

I grab the towel from the sink and dry off. I look even more tired than I did before we left today. The hollows beneath my eyes seem bigger, somehow. I lean forward, looking at them. They're more pronounced, aren't they?

I dry off and change into something comfortable. Dinner is in an hour.

The jaguar comes back to mind, and I go over it

again. But after that, I'm left with the memory of Collin in the jungle. How he'd looked confused when I'd told him I must have told Cece about their divorce.

What are you talking about?

If I didn't tell her about the divorce papers, what were they fighting about?

Maybe she already knew on her own. Maybe that's what he meant.

But if I didn't tell her, there's no reason for Collin to have wanted to hurt me, is there?

He'd asked me again what I remember. There's some reason he's stuck on that. What does he hope I *don't* remember? What did I see?

What happened before I went overboard?

"We should probably head down," Steve says.

I've been staring out the window while he's been reading for the last forty-five minutes, I realize. The time passed in a flash. I wonder if I've been thinking about that interaction the whole time. I don't normally zone out so intensely.

Could it be the head injury?

"Right," I say, getting up from the window.

When we get downstairs, Collin and Cece are already seated, both of them with a drink in hand.

I smile at them both as I sit down and inwardly cringe when Steve says he's going to go get us both something to drink. I'd rather he not leave me alone with them.

"How was your afternoon?" I ask, nervously smiling at the pair of them.

"Good," Collin says. "How are you?"

"I'm fine," I say. "Nothing like two near-death experi-ences on one vacation." I hope that I'll get a laugh out of the pair of them, but Collin only smirks slightly. Cece says nothing.

Collin's eyes linger on me, like he wants to ask me more questions.

Suddenly, I'm praying that Cece will acknowledge me and take the conversation by the reins.

She does no such thing.

"It's been a good trip despite it," I remark to no one in particular.

They both seem preoccupied and finally, to my immense relief, Steve comes back with an alcoholic drink for each of us.

"You've earned it," he says, handing me an amaretto sour.

"Thank you," I say.

I don't dare raise a glass, and I thank God that Steve doesn't, either.

Steve manages to make small talk, but that tension is still there. Something isn't right.

Things seem to cool as dinner arrives. Maybe just the fact that everyone's stomachs are full has eased things a bit. I'm tempted to remind them all that we have several days left on a boat together, but fight the urge.

"I think we're going to go to the game room after dinner," Collin says, clearing his throat.

"Have fun," Steve says, not offering for us to join. "I think we'll call it an early night."

Shortly afterward, Collin and Cece get up from the

table and head toward the other end of the boat where the game room is. I imagine them gambling in a smoky room with other passengers over poker and roulette.

Once we're alone, Steve relaxes back into his chair and puts an arm around me.

"Shall we?" he asks, squeezing my shoulder.

I nod, but as Steve stands up and starts to walk toward the staircase, I notice something in Collin's seat.

The green motel-style keychain bearing their room number.

He must have dropped it out of his pocket when they got up to go to the game room.

I should take it to them.

I glance at Steve. He's almost to the winding little staircase. I swipe the keychain off the leather chair and stuff it into my bra. I scurry along, following Steve up the steps.

Inside the room, we undress and get ready for bed.

I bide my time and wait until he's snoring peacefully. I reach over and make sure that his phone is silenced. The last thing I need is him waking up and realizing I'm not in here.

I silence my own phone and then go over to my suitcase where I stuffed the key after changing for bed. And then I sneak out into the hallway, being ever so careful to close our door as quietly as possible. I squint my eyes when the door creaks as it closes completely. I strain my ears and hear Steve snoring, then sigh in relief.

The hallway is empty and the open balcony at the end of it looks out over the dark night on the Amazon. I glance at the space between the carpet and the door of Collin and Cece's room. It's dark. No light on inside. And there's only one key to each room. They couldn't have gotten in without it.

I slip it into the lock and turn it. The door opens without protest.

Stepping into the darkened room, I feel out of place. The strong sense that I'm doing something I shouldn't comes over me. I feel like they could catch me at any moment.

I close the door behind me and flip on the light switch.

The room is identical to ours. Only different clothing and personal items are strewn about the room. Where Steve has kept ours tidy, Collin and Cece seem to have let their luggage explode. It surprises me a little bit.

For some reason, I'd imagined them neat as a pin.

Standing there, I realize I've just intruded into their space. It's not something I've ever done before. I've never even been the kind of wife to go through her husband's phone, but I've done that in the last twenty-four hours, too.

I feel like I'm losing my grip on reality.

Walking around the room, I take in my surroundings. An empty glass on the nightstand and something beside it, reflecting the light with a little sparkle. I look closer and walk toward the nightstand.

It's Cece's wedding ring.

Like she only just took it off and left it there today. I wonder if she just forgot it, or if there's a more sinister reason why she's not wearing it. Collin looked so confused when I brought up the divorce papers.

I glance around the room again. Both of their suitcases sit on the floor of the closet. Some garments are hung carefully above, but others are still folded inside their luggage. Others, already worn, are strewn about the closet floor.

I walk into the bathroom, unsure of what I'm even looking for at this point. I flip on the light switch and look down at the sink, and immediately I see it.

Steve's button.

From his shirt.

I think of the vision of Steve just after I settled in the infirmary, his shirt hanging slightly open. I pick up the little gold button and flip it over in my palm, feeling its smooth edge beneath my thumb. Thinking again about the other night, I wonder where the button came off. Why would it be in here? Like someone picked it up and saved it? Why would anyone do that?

I tuck it into the pocket of my pajama pants and go back out into their room. Glancing at the clock, I realize it's close to one in the morning. They're going to be coming back any time now, and Collin will realize he doesn't have his key.

There's the danger that someone working for the cruise line will let him in with a master key. They could walk in on me, wandering around their room. It would only make things worse.

What am I looking for?

I couldn't tell you. Something. Anything. Anything

that will point me in the right direction about what happened to me. About what happened before we got on this boat.

There's a desk against the wall, and I walk over to it. A cell phone rests, plugged into its charger. I tap the screen and an image of Collin and Cece on their wedding day brightens the screen. Swiping up from the bottom, I'm met with the prompt to enter the passcode.

I stare at it for a moment and do something that I'm positive is a shot in the dark.

0000

I read once that so many people use simple codes for things they shouldn't.

Not expecting anything, I'm shocked when the phone's security lets me in. I stare at the screen for a moment, unsure that I've done what I think I have. Apps dot the screen and I grab the phone, immediately heading for the web browser. I navigate to the history.

Nowhere in it do I find a search for anything that would lead to the Smith and Turner lawyers.

Collin could have covered his tracks. With a passcode that easy, I'm not sure he'd leave evidence that Cece could easily get access to. I wonder if he usually guards his phone carefully, not leaving it where she might get a chance to snoop through it. Maybe, he thought, since they were going down to dinner together, then to the casino, the phone was safe to leave charging up here.

I struggle to figure out the logic, and remind myself I don't really have time for that.

I start snooping through his phone, looking for what, I'm not sure.

But it's when I open the Files folder on it that I find something.

A folder labeled *Future*.

Inside, there are several documents. I open one and it's the itinerary for the trip we're on. Another is a packing list. One is the cost of the trip. And finally, I find a spreadsheet with a bunch of numbers on it. There are two long numbers at the top and then a column of smaller numbers with decimal points running down the page.

I navigate to the Mail app and attach the document. Then I send it to myself. I clear it out of the Send box and erase any obvious signs that I sent myself something from Collin's phone. I lock it and put it back down on the table, and then I scurry out into the hallway. At the last second, I decide to place the keychain on the ground right in front of the door.

Then I head back to our room.

When I crawl into bed, I check to make sure the email came through. It did.

Steve rolls over in his sleep and wraps an arm around me, pulling me tight.

"Put that away," he murmurs.

Reluctantly, I lock my phone and put it back over on the nightstand.

I stare at my phone as Steve's breath fans across my shoulder, and I realize it's going to have to wait until tomorrow for me to get a look at the spreadsheet. In the meantime, my mind returns to the button and I reach down, feeling it in my pocket, making sure it's real, and it's there.

Why would this button be in that bathroom?

The question circulates around in my mind and I ruminate about it until I fall asleep around four in the morning.

And it's right around then that I hear a voice in the hallway.

"There it is!"

Then I hear the door next to ours open and close as our companions return to their room for the night, none the wiser that I've betrayed whatever trust there was between us.

SEVENTEEN

IN THE MORNING, I reach for my phone as soon as Steve gets up to use the bathroom. Quickly, I open the document I emailed to myself and scan through the numbers again, trying to make sense of them. Nothing is labeled. It's nonsensical, and I imagine the only person that could make anything of it is Collin. I'm not keen on asking for his help.

I lock my phone and my mind returns to the button.

Maybe one of them noticed it somewhere and picked it up, meaning to give it back to Steve.

Such a small thing to notice, though.

Steve emerges from the bathroom and I lay my phone on my stomach, smiling up at him.

"Good morning," he says with a grin, and climbs back into bed next to me.

"Good morning," I say.

"What's on the agenda today?" he asks.

I look over at him and shrug my shoulders.

"No excursions where I might get killed?" I suggest.

He chuckles and grabs my hand, kissing the back of it.

It was so stupid to assume the worst when I picked up his phone the other night. Steve is in love with me. We always have been. Ever since we met. Even when we were both taken. We knew it the moment we laid eyes on each other.

That feels so long ago now.

I tuck my head against his shoulder and snuggle down beside him. Not wanting to leave the room, I pull the covers up to my chin and he relaxes against me.

"Maybe we could just keep to ourselves today," I suggest, more seriously now.

He kisses the top of my head as though he's happy with the suggestion.

"That sounds quite nice," he says.

"We're happy, aren't we?" I ask after a beat of silence.

Memories of times gone by dance through my head. How we met, fell in love, and what we both left behind to be together. Neither of us would ever risk that again. I look up at him.

"Of course," he says. "Why would you ask that?"

"Just making sure," I say.

"You're thinking about that phone call the other night, aren't you?"

"No," I insist. I shrug, trying to feign nonchalance.

But that *is* what I'm thinking about.

"I promise you that if I wanted a divorce, you'd be the first person to know about it," Steve says, his tone teasing.

"I'm serious, Steve."

I lean up on my elbow and look at him.

"Our marriage is good, isn't it?"

He searches my face for whatever meaning there might be in my question. Realization seems to dawn on him and immediately I wonder if I've pushed my luck too far.

"You really hit your head hard, didn't you?" He asks with a small laugh. There's no mirth in it.

I lay back down against him, not eager to follow the conversation through to its logical destination.

I should just tell him.

Why can I tell him that I don't remember anything?

I should.

But there's a niggling little doubt in the back of my mind telling me to keep it to myself.

Not just yet.

The fact that it's even there gives me pause. I remember reading once that when you have a gut feeling of fear, you should listen to it. It's telling you something that your conscious mind isn't aware of.

I think about being in the jungle, staring down an animal that could have killed me as easily as looked at me. The way it seemed to study me. How I hadn't been aware of its presence until it made the mistake of breaking a branch.

Otherwise, I might not have known she was there until it was too late.

The thought swims in my mind and I want to drown it.

"I'm sorry," I say to Steve, snuggling back against him. Though this time his body feels rigid against mine. The softness that was there is gone now.

"It's alright," he says in a tone that would sound reassuring to anyone that didn't know what he actually sounds like when he's being reassuring. The note of falsity in it makes me uneasy.

What's he thinking?

I wonder what I would find if I could read his mind.

Just then, there's a knock at the door.

Steve sits up, dragging his arm from beneath my head. I don't want to get up, and I find myself annoyed that housekeeping would knock on the door this early.

He goes over and opens it.

"Wondered if the two of you might like to get mimosas," Collin says from the hallway.

I immediately turn, craning my neck that way.

He looks like he hasn't slept, and he catches me gawking at him. There's an intensity to his eyes. I wonder if they spent the night fighting. If maybe inviting us to breakfast is his attempt to not have to bear the brunt of Cece's wrath on his own. Steve and I might provide a much-needed buffer if that's the case.

I sit up on the bed, hoping that Steve will tell him no. That we're planning on taking it easy today. He casts a glance back at me and frustration is etched on his face. Like he feels a loyalty to Collin but doesn't want to act on it. Like he'd rather do just as we'd planned. I offer him a smile, accepting our fate. He turns to Collin.

"Sure. Let us get changed."

Collin nods.

"I'll wait for you guys out here," he says, his voice strained.

I imagine him and Cece, whisper fighting so they don't wake anyone on the boat. So they don't make a scene.

Or maybe so we don't hear what they're fighting about.

I think about the spreadsheet of numbers.

Steve closes the door.

"I'll get changed and freshened up and then it's your turn," he says, grabbing a shirt and shorts and disappearing into the bathroom. I nod and smile, but immediately go back to my phone.

I look at the spreadsheet again.

And a number on it seems familiar.

1212.

The number is listed twice. One right after another.

Why does that seem familiar?

My brain rolls it over and over again. I know that number. It means something.

Where have I seen that?

"Your turn," Steve says when he exits the bathroom, nearly making me jump out of my skin. I fumble my cell phone onto the floor.

"Jesus fucking Christ!" I hiss.

He laughs at me.

"Jumpy much?" he teases.

I stoop down and grab my phone, locking it and putting it on the nightstand so I can get up and get dressed. Playfully, I punch Steve in his arm on my way to the bathroom. I change and we start to head out into the hall.

And then Steve's phone rings.

"Shit, I gotta take this," he says when he glances at it. "I'll be right out. You don't have to wait for me. Go on down."

As if that's some sort of privilege.

"I'll wait for you," I tell him.

"No," he says firmly. "I insist. Go down."

There's an intensity in his eyes.

He doesn't want me to listen to this phone call.

Suddenly, a knot of dread forms in my gut. Is it the divorce attorneys? Why wouldn't he want me to overhear the call if it was what he said it was? If it's for Collin, what does it matter?

I hesitate at the door, but before he picks up, he gestures for me to leave.

I feel like a child being dismissed by her father.

Obediently, but reluctantly, I go out into the darkened hallway. Morning light spills in through either open end of the boat and on the balcony, I spot Collin. No Cece.

I want to snake around him and down the stairs without him noticing. I can't decide which would be worse, being alone with Cece again or facing another awkward interaction with Collin.

I glance back at our door, hoping that Steve might step out at any second, but he doesn't.

Nervously, I walk toward the staircase, trying to make

as little noise as possible, but just as I'm about to reach it, a board creaks and Collin spins, almost like he's been caught doing something he shouldn't.

"I didn't hear you come out," he says, and then a smile breaks across his face. Almost like he's relieved it's just me and not Steve.

It fills me with the uneasiness that's becoming so familiar on this trip.

I smile back, trying to project confidence.

"Just me," I say in return. Reaching for the railing, I take one step down.

Collin places his hand over mine, stopping me.

"Why did you think Cece and I were getting a divorce?" he asks.

Cutting right to the chase, he gives me no time to be any more nervous. My eyes dart around, hoping that I'll see someone that can intervene. Or at least interrupt us.

But there's no one.

It's just us.

"I don't know. I guess that was silly of me. Maybe hitting my head made me confused. I'm sorry," I say. I blurt it all out.

"Why did we come on this trip?" Collin asks.

The question is so strange that I fight the urge to ask him if he's high.

There's an intensity to his gaze that threatens me and assures me I should tell the truth.

"Relaxation?" My voice comes out as barely a whimper.

He lets go of my wrist.

Just as I'm about to run down the staircase, I get the idea to seize this opportunity and ask him a strange question.

"Collin," I say. "Did you pick up a button from Steve's shirt the other night?"

"What? No," he says. Looking confused, he stares at me like I've asked him the weirdest question he's ever heard. Like the ones he's been asking me haven't been off the wall, too. "Why?" he asks.

I swallow.

"No reason," I say.

I start down the staircase, and he grabs my wrist.

"They were arguing," he says.

"What?" I ask, turning to face him. "Who?"

"The two of them. Just before you fell," he adds. "They were fighting. And then you went overboard."

"What are you saying?"

Collin looks at me like he's waiting for me to put it all together. And then realization dawns on me.

The button in their room. A fight between Steve and Cece. The divorce attorney.

Our relationship started as a lie.

Why couldn't his next?

EIGHTEEN

"I WOULD DO ANYTHING FOR YOU."

Barely a whisper, the words almost echoed off the walls.

He was out of town for the weekend and you came over, snuck in, and we had sex in the bed he paid for.

It felt like blasphemy for you to say those words in his rooms. And that was what delighted me about it. Never once then did I think that I might live and die by the sword.

You kissed me and pulled away, laughing.

"I can't wait until all of this is gone," you gestured toward the room. "Until you're all mine and I can have you any time I want you."

I laughed coyly, trying to put off more conversations about the future. The planning hurt me because it felt like it would never come to fruition. Any time you were about to leave her, something would come up and I'd be devastated all over again.

I'd decided that I wasn't going to get my hopes up. If it was going to happen, it would happen.

"We could go away together," you suggested.

I laughed.

"Someday," I said.

"One day soon," you insisted. You leaned up on your elbow and kissed the back of my hand. "You know I'd do anything for you, right?"

"Leave your wife?"

The words came out even though I'd meant to only think them. I think they'd been sitting there in the back of my throat, biding their time for the right moment to sting.

You looked hurt, but you didn't deny me my barb.

You knew it was valid.

"I'd do more than that," you said. "Anything. Anything at all. And we will be together," you assured me. "After everything is in order. It's just a matter of time."

I said nothing.

I was so naïve to have fallen in love with you. My life was good. There was nothing wrong with it. I was comfortable and taken care of. I had a husband that loved me and a house to come home to and make my own. I should have told you to go fuck yourself right then and there.

We wouldn't be in this mess now if I had.

But there was something about you that always kept me coming back. That kept me from letting go completely. No matter how much you hurt me with your broken promises.

I looked over at you and reached for your face. I traced

the chiseled outline of your jaw and touched the hard line of your lips. You kissed my fingertip.

"I would do anything for you, too," I said.

"Leave him?" you asked, echoing my question from earlier.

I smiled.

"Whenever you're ready," I said.

"Soon," you assured me.

That spring passed and the two of us saw each other more and more frequently. At one point, we had to slow down, both of us feeling that if we continued at that pace, our spouses would grow suspicious.

Every meeting felt like something out of a mob movie. The two of us pulling up next to each other in abandoned strip mall parking lots. Meeting behind your gym before it opened, having slipped out of bed claiming I was going to work out. Each of us arriving separately at the bookstore and then browsing together, talking quietly, and hoping that we weren't drawing attention to ourselves.

When we backed off, I realized how much I missed you.

I realized that I did want this to happen sooner rather than later.

I was ready to leave him.

NINETEEN

RATTLED, I try to shake Collin off, rushing down the steps toward the dining area. He follows close behind, though, periodically reaching for my arm. I jerk away as he tries to slow me down.

"Stop," I spin and say as we reach the downstairs landing.

He holds both hands up in mock surrender.

"Stephanie," he says.

I head on toward our table and quickly take my seat, hoping that being in the middle of the crowded deck will make him watch what he says. I don't want to talk about this. It's absurd, isn't it? I bark out a laugh as he sits.

"So, what?" I ask. "You're saying this is some elaborate conspiracy between your wife and my husband to get rid of me?"

He stares at me, a sadness in his eyes.

"No," he says. "That's not what I'm saying."

"Then what *are* you saying?"

"I just think you need to watch your back and we need to make it through this trip," he says. "With all of us on board this boat when we dock in a few days."

I stare at him for a moment, trying to read his face.

What's he not telling me?

"Do you think they're having an affair?" I ask.

"Maybe," he says with a shrug.

"Why else would one of them shove me overboard?" I ask. "Things have been off for a while," I mutter to myself, thinking about the fuzzy tension I remember from just before the trip.

"Do you remember being shoved?" His eyebrow arches.

Frustrated, I lean my forehead against my palms, elbows resting on the table.

"I remember the sensation of being pushed, yes," I say.

"Does Steve know that?" he asks.

I choke out a little laugh.

"Of course," I lie.

I look up and Collin's staring at me.

"No, he doesn't," Collin says with assurance.

I find myself shaking my head, admitting that I've kept this from my husband.

"How much do you not remember, Stephanie?"

"A lot," I say, a sob in my throat. I realize how vulnerable I am right now and rub my face, not wanting to cry in front of Collin. "What about you? All *this*," I gesture to the space between us—the conversation we're having.

"Why should I trust you? I shouldn't even be talking about this with you."

Collin seems to think about this, and then he leans forward across the table, hands clasped and his eyes boring into mine.

"It wouldn't be the first time you told me Steve hurt you," he says.

It feels like he's splashed ice cold water over me.

"What?" I ask with a laugh.

He seems to be carefully choosing his words.

"Yeah, a little over a month ago," Collin says. "I was at the office late. You came up there to get something for him. You didn't realize I was there." He looks away from me, almost like recalling it is painful for him. I furrow my brow, listening as this practical stranger fills in the blanks of my memory. "You were crying," he goes on. "Sobbing, really. And you walked into the office and made a beeline for his office. I stepped out to check on you and you jumped when you saw me. I flipped on the light in the entry hall. Your face was red and your eye puffy, with the beginnings of a bruise. He'd given you a black eye, even if it hadn't totally shown up yet. I recognized it because my dad used to give those to my mom."

I flinch at his words.

The idea that Steve could hit me is so foreign. But then I think about everything else that's going on. What if I knew about the affair and confronted him? What if I had threatened to take everything, and he'd lost his temper?

I say nothing, waiting for Collin to go on, and he does.

"You were so startled. You looked terrified. I'd seen that look on my mom's face. I asked you what had happened, and you just melted into a puddle of tears right in front of me. You said he'd hit you."

"Because I knew," I fill in the blank.

Collin nods.

"Is that why Cece is so uptight?" I ask.

"I confronted her the first night we were here," Collin says. "I wanted to wait until after the trip, but I couldn't."

"Christ," I mutter. Then I laugh. "I should have known this would happen."

"Why?" Collin asks.

"Steve and I began our own relationship as an affair. We were both married," I say. "I remember this one time when we were out, sneaking around. We'd been at the zoo when Jane had called. Jane was his first wife," I say.

Collin opens his mouth to speak and then stops short.

I've said too much. He doesn't want to hear all the sordid details that led to this.

"I hope I'm not interrupting anything," Steve says from behind me.

I jump, just like I did in Collin's story.

"Not at all," I say too quickly. "Sit."

Collin leans back, the intensity between us dissipating in a moment. Just after he shows up, Cece follows. I wonder if they were talking.

Plotting. Planning their exit just like Steve and I had.

I catch her looking at him. I glance at Collin and he

clears his throat, aware of it, too. Cece looks away, back at her own husband, though she says nothing.

"Where are the mimosas?" Steve asks, somewhat playfully. There's an undercurrent of tension in the question. Like he's asking why Collin and I haven't already procured them. Have we been talking this whole time? It's almost like he asks out loud.

"I'll get them," I say, standing from the table and leaving the three of them to it.

I try to absorb the shock of the information that Collin just shared with me.

A black eye.

Christ.

Steve has always had a temper, but he'd never hit me before.

He'd also never shoved me over the railing of a second-story balcony before.

He's lying about the divorce attorney. *He* called them. *He* wanted me gone when he realized it would be too expensive to do it legally.

A chill runs through me.

And I have no means of escape.

I stand at the bar, watching as the bartender gathers the glasses for the four of us.

"How are you holding up?"

I turn, shocked to see Cece standing beside me.

"Fine," I tell her, suddenly feeling the urge to be frosty. "You?"

"Fine," she says. "Thought I'd help you carry the glasses."

I bite back the urge to ask her why my husband's button was on her bathroom sink. I can't believe it. All this time, I thought Steve and I were pulling one over on everyone else, and that wasn't the case at all. I'd been lulled into a false sense of security.

Had she ripped off his button in the heat of passion? Kept it as a souvenir? The thought is disgusting, and I'm aware of the irony.

We stand there in an awkward silence as the bartender pours the mimosas more slowly than I think any bartender ever has in the history of time.

Finally, he hands them to us. She takes two and I take two.

"Cece," I say, right as she's about to start back for the table. She looks up at me. "He'll leave you for someone else."

She looks at me like I've slapped her.

"What did you say?"

"Don't let him fool you," I say. "All those pretty lies are just a pile of shit in the morning light. So, get your shovel."

And with that, I head back to our table.

TWENTY

I GET Steve to stop hovering over me for the rest of the day and make it my mission to spend as much time alone as I can, without the annoyance of them in my presence. Finally, as the sun sets, I come in from the balcony and close the magazine I've been flipping through all day. Too wound up to focus on a book, flipping through a travel mag while fantasizing about being anywhere but here was just the ticket.

"Do you not want to go to dinner?" Steve asks when I come in.

"I think I'll pass," I say. "But you go."

My tone is dismissive, and he catches it.

"What's wrong, Steph?" he asks.

"Why did we come on this trip?" I ask.

He furrows his brows, puzzled.

"Because you wanted to," he says, the statement going up in octave at the end like a question. Like I'm trying to trick him somehow.

"Were we having problems?" I press.

At this point, I don't really care how vulnerable it makes me. I want to hear it from him.

He shakes his head.

"Problems?" he asks. "What are you talking about?" He adds the last with a half-smile, like he can't believe I'd ask such a thing.

I don't return the expression.

"Problems, you know?" I say, unable to bring myself to articulate exactly what it is I'm asking. It occurs to me the position I'm putting myself in. But I feel like I don't really have any choice. I can't just let it go.

"We've had our share," Steve says. "But nothing serious."

He stares at me, his eyes fixed on my face, like he's looking for some micro-expression that might tell him what I'm getting at.

"You know, I always used to think it was us against the world," I say, feeling a lump form in my throat. I hate how much I don't want to lose him. It's such a far cry from the girl I used to be. Losing Steve doesn't conjure feelings of freedom. Losing Steve conjures feelings of emptiness and failure. "But it feels like there's a world between us right now."

Steve furrows his brow, and a sad laugh escapes his mouth. He smiles halfheartedly.

"I'm not wrong, am I?" I ask.

Steve is my one great love, and I don't know if I've realized that until just now.

The idea that I was just a steppingstone to his next

affair is enough to turn my stomach. Enough to keep me from eating for a solid year.

That thought makes me realize that maybe we aren't the same.

Maybe we didn't mean the same things when we made all those promises.

"You are wrong," he says.

He steps forward toward me and takes both of my hands. He looks down at them as he gathers his thoughts, then finally, he looks me in the eye, his expression warm.

"There is nothing you could ever do that would make me love you less, and I love you more with each passing moment. I've never known a woman like you, Stephanie. The way you command a room, your passion, the way your eyes light up when you get a mischievous thought." He smiles. "I couldn't ever imagine doing life without you."

The tears are falling freely now.

Steve steps closer and takes my chin in his hand. He presses his lips to mine, kissing me slowly, softly. Like I'm the love of his life. And I know he's the love of mine.

Steve pulls away.

"We don't need to go down to dinner," he says, reaching up and brushing hair out of my face.

"Good," I say. "I'm a mess." I laugh.

Steve orders room service for us and we snuggle up in bed with our food. We watch a movie, and after we're done, Steve turns out the lights and we open the balcony door. The night air comes in, warm and humid, but it's nice. A gentle reminder that there's life outside these walls. That soon we'll go home, and things can get back to normal.

But there's one thing bothering me.

Collin's story.

How can I trust a man that hit me?

I can't remember another time that Steve had unpredictable anger. Never before that in our marriage had he put his hands on me. It's a deal breaker for me. I would never stay in such a situation.

But even as I have that thought, I think about the women I've known who *did* stay and how many extenuating circumstances play into whether you can actually get out of that nightmare or not. It's not as simple as saying you'd never let it happen to you.

I snuggle up against Steve, pushing thoughts of violence to the back of my mind.

What if no one pushed me? What if that memory isn't right?

Why does Collin think his wife and my husband are having an affair?

Maybe she's mad at him because it's not true and he insists that it is.

There's only one thing that I need to know the truth about.

But then Steve gives me the perfect opening.

"What were you and Collin talking about earlier?" he asks.

"He told me a story, actually," I say. "Family stuff. It was a little strange that he shared it, but he said his dad used to beat up his mom. I don't even remember how we got on that."

Steve snorts with a bitter laugh.

"He must have been pulling your leg," he says.

"No one would joke about something like that!" I say.

Steve starts to laugh.

"Collin never knew his mother. She died when he was born," he says. "Sometimes he has a strange sense of humor," he adds. "I guess he got you."

Stunned into silence, I lay beside my husband.

Collin lied to me.

Why the *fuck* would he lie about that?

And why would he tell me that Steve had hit me?

What in the hell is going on?

TWENTY-ONE

FINALLY, I find my voice.

"I need you to look at something," I say, sitting up in bed and grabbing my phone. I navigate to the spreadsheet and hand it to Steve. "What is this?"

Steve takes the phone and squints as his eyes adjust to the bright light in the darkness.

He scrolls through the spreadsheet, looking at each number. I watch his face carefully, wondering what he's making of it.

"It looks like it might be expenses? Or deposits?" It comes out as more of a question than a statement. He long presses on one of the cells and checks the formatting, something I hadn't thought to do. "They're monetary amounts."

Money.

Why would Collin lie to me about my husband hurting me?

"What is this?" Steve asks.

"I found it on Collin's phone," I say.

Steve's eyes open wide.

"Why did you have Collin's phone?" He sits up straight in bed.

"I think he shoved me overboard," I say.

Steve's expression changes from one of confusion to one of horror.

"Oh, my God," he says slowly. "Hang on."

He grabs his own phone and navigates to the banking app for the business. I watch over his shoulder as he does so. He scrolls through a number of transactions.

"Oh, my God. All of these numbers are charges that were invoiced to another company. Black Label Trading. I have no idea who that is," he says.

I grab my phone and bring up the Secretary of State's website for California. I search the business.

The registration information appears on the screen, and the name shocks me into silence.

I have no idea what this means, and I stare at the screen, willing the words to be something different. Someone different.

The name on the screen is my own.

"WHY IS that registered in my name?" I ask Steve, horrified.

My hand shakes as I hand him my phone. He stares at it, taking it in just like I did. Like he can't believe what he's seeing. I want to tell him I feel the same way, but I'm too stunned to say much else.

"Did you register a company?" Steve asks, turning serious.

"Of course not! I would know, wouldn't I?"

The rhetorical question hangs between us, not all that rhetorical.

"Of course," Steve says. He mutters to himself, inaudible to me. "I'm sure you didn't do this," he says conclusively.

I don't press it, asking him how he's so sure. I just want him to know it beyond a shadow of a doubt. That's good enough for me right now.

"It looks like he's hiding money," Steve says. Then, to himself, "I guess it's worse than I thought."

"You thought this was going on?" I ask.

"No, no. That's not what I meant," he says quickly. "Just—I've had a feeling something like this was happening," he says, somewhat sadly. "Remember when you couldn't find your passport or your wallet?" he asks.

I don't. It's part of that hazy month leading up to the trip, but I take his word for it.

"I'm sure he registered it in your name and opened an account. He would have had all the information he'd need to do so. You can register a business online. And you can open a bank account the same way."

Despite the horror that Collin is embezzling, I feel relief.

"Why would he use my name?" I ask.

"Probably so that if I looked into it, I wouldn't jump to any conclusions," Steve says. "Shit."

He hands my phone back to me. I stare at the spreadsheet.

"Don't worry," he says. "I'll take care of it."

The way he says it chills me. There's a coldness to his tone that I hadn't expected. I think about all the times he's said he'd do anything for me. I wonder now what that included. How far *anything* really went.

"Don't do anything stupid," I tell him.

Steve is quiet for a moment.

"Did you confront him about this?" Steve asks.

"What? No!"

"Steph, what if you can't remember? What if you found out about this and confronted him out here? What if he shoved you overboard because you'd stumbled onto this?" Steve says.

I shake my head back and forth. What if that's what happened?

What if I stumbled onto some of this information last month? What if some argument made it come to a head the other night?

And then Collin just decided he'd get rid of me.

And now he's been trying to drive a wedge between me and Steve, hoping that distance would keep me from telling him the things I know. Hoping that it would make me mistrust my own husband.

That's why he said Steve hurt me.

It's a chilling realization.

"I think that must have happened," I say.

"He pushed you," Steve says, incredulous.

"What do we do now?" I ask.

I feel lost, looking to Steve for how to get out of this situation.

"We need to make it through the rest of the trip. Act like everything's normal. Like neither of us know a thing, Steph."

I nod solemnly. He's right.

"Okay," I say.

"We only have two days left, and then we're getting off the boat and heading to Iquitos," he says. "After that, we fly back to Lima and home to Los Angeles. And then I'll sort this out."

I nod again, unsure if there's anything else I can do. I feel so lost, so vulnerable. Like I've been involved in something criminal against my will.

"In Iquitos, we'll just stay at the hotel. We won't go on the retreat. They can go without us," Steve says.

"Retreat?" I ask.

"An ayahuasca retreat. I don't think it would be wise given your head injury," Steve says. "I also don't think it would be wise to mix drugs with the current situation."

I nod again, agreeing with Steve.

The last thing I want is to make things worse, and the idea of taking a psychedelic on top of everything sounds disastrous.

Steve and I are quiet for a moment, and then I put my phone back on the nightstand. He does the same.

"Can we just go back to how things were a minute ago?" I ask, sounding younger and more scared than I mean to.

"Of course," he says, pulling me next to him in the

darkness. The balcony is still open, the moon reflecting off the river. I hear a howler monkey cry somewhere in the jungle. I snuggle closer to Steve, placing my hand on his chest and my head on his shoulder. I inhale the scent of him and think of home.

And even though I try to relax, I can't shake the distinct feeling that there's some piece of this whole puzzle that I'm missing.

TWENTY-TWO

IT WAS *early summer when you asked me.*

"Is it time?" I asked.

I'd been ready for some time. And now we were finally making plans to leave them. He had no idea, and I don't think she did, either.

I remember we met at the same Starbucks where it had all started.

You ordered the same thing you had that first day, and I did, too. The Americano steamed, and I wondered how anyone could drink such a thing in this heat. I sipped from my bottle of Ethos, grateful that it was cold and not just cool.

"How have you been?" you asked.

It had been a while since we'd gotten to meet like this. Both of us trying to keep up appearances had taken its toll on our stolen moments. I smiled at you, still taken with your charm.

"I've been good," I said.

"You look good," you'd commented. "Beautiful as ever."

"Oh, hush," I said, taking a sip of my water. "Drink your coffee."

You blushed and looked down with a grin, then back up at me.

"I'm ready whenever you are," you said.

We made our plans to tell them that night. And then from there, we'd meet at the Roosevelt. I'd always wanted to stay there.

But that night, when I got home, when I looked at him, so comfortable in our marriage, I couldn't do it. And before I could text you to tell you that, you'd already sent a message asking for another day.

I sighed, looking at my phone, and wondering if either of us would ever have the constitution necessary to get us to the Roosevelt.

TWENTY-THREE

THE NEXT DAY passes without much fanfare. I do my best to keep to myself, or make sure Steve is with me whenever I'm out of the room. The last thing I want is to be alone with Collin after Steve telling me that he lied about his mother.

Such a strange thing to lie about, I think.

And it sends my mind in all different directions, wondering what his end game was with that. I keep coming back to the idea that he wanted to drive a wedge between me and Steve. He wanted some kind of wiggle room in there. Maybe to keep either of us from communicating enough to realize that Collin had pushed me.

Just like us, he's in survival mode until we reach the end of the cruise.

The day after that, I find myself downstairs alone. Steve leaves momentarily just to go back up to the room because he forgot something. Dread overcomes me as I sit in the dining area by myself. Collin and Cece haven't come down yet, but I'm afraid they'll make it before Steve gets back. The thought makes me squirm in my chair. I remind myself, though, that Collin isn't as likely to engage me in a weird conversation if Cece's with him.

So when I see the two of them descend the stairs together, I breathe a sigh of relief. Even if Steve isn't with me, at least I'm not alone with Collin. I force a smile at the two of them as they take their seats.

"Good morning," Collin says, offering me a smile that seems genuine.

It makes me wonder what really *is* genuine about him.

I rack my brain, scrolling through my memories like you might a Rolodex. I'm looking for that moment that I must have confronted him, but I don't find it. Damn, I wish I could bring it to mind, because I think it's the key to unlocking everything.

So much of my memories from the last month are hazy and I feel like if I could remember just one solid thing, it would unravel the rest.

"Good morning," I say.

"Morning," Cece says, sounding like she'd rather be in bed right now than down here with us. "Excuse me."

She stands from the table, and my eyes follow her as she leaves. I find myself wanting to call out to her, to beg her to stay. But I don't. I remain silent and turn my focus back to Collin. I give him a nervous chuckle.

"Just the two of us," I say, crossing my arms over my chest like that might somehow protect me.

"Just the two of us," he repeats. "So, are the two of

you still game for the ayahuasca retreat tomorrow night after we arrive in Iquitos?"

The question catches me off guard, but at least it's one I know the answer to.

"I don't think we're going to join you. Steve doesn't think it's a good idea with my injury and all," I say, giving Collin a little frown, trying to indicate that we give them our best.

"That might be a good reason to go through with it," he suggests.

My brow furrows.

"I hardly think mixing a psychedelic with a cheese-cloth memory is a good idea," I say somewhat firmly.

"You never know. You might remember something you didn't plan on," he says.

I consider this for a moment. What if he's right?

"You know," he says. "Studies have been done on psychedelics and the mind. There's a good chance that you actually *might* remember something you can't right now."

He leans forward as he says it, that same intensity he had the other day. I don't like it, and I lean back, away from him.

Even still, I think there might be some merit to what he's saying.

What if I *could* conjure a complete memory?

What if the whole of last month came back to me?

"People have been using psychedelics to treat mental health concerns for a long time," Collin assures me. "And I feel like memory would be no different. What if the neural pathways you've used to access your memories have been damaged? What if the ayahuasca could find an alternate path?"

I stare at him, considering this.

"Good morning," Steve says stiffly.

He sits down beside me.

"What are you two talking about?" he asks, trying to sound as nonchalant as possible, but I hear the strain in his voice.

"The ayahuasca retreat," Collin says. "I was just suggesting that you two should consider joining us."

"I don't think that's a good idea with Steph's head injury," Steve says, sounding like an authority on the matter.

"Wait," I say, touching him on the arm. "I think—well, Collin was just saying it might be beneficial for my memory," I tell him.

He looks over at Collin, seeming to eye him suspiciously. Then he looks at me, his tone turning gentle.

"I really don't think that's a wise idea," he says.

I stare at him, imploring him to see the logic behind the idea.

What if I could remember everything? Wouldn't that benefit us when we get back home?

Steve glances over at Collin, apparently not getting the memo so clearly written on my face.

"Thanks, though," he says, as though the matter is closed.

"Just consider it," Collin insists.

"We have," Steve says. "She's not going. Neither of us are."

I feel like a kid being told that the plans I made with my friend aren't going to work out after all, or that our trip to Disney World has just been canceled. I sigh.

After Cece returns, we all have breakfast, and I excuse myself to the room. I drag Steve with me, and as soon as the door closes, I start in on him.

"I think it might actually be a good idea," I tell him.

"What?" he asks, unsure what I'm talking about since it's been an hour since we were talking about the ayahuasca retreat.

"The psychedelics. The ayahuasca," I say.

"Oh, Steph. No way," he says, shaking his head.

"I think we should think about it," I insist.

I can see that we're at a crossroads. He doesn't want to consider this. His mind is already made up.

"Just consider it, please," I say.

There's the hint of a threat in my tone, though. Steve knows me. I'm not one to be told what to do, and if there's something I really want, I go after it.

"Do you think it's a good idea to listen to Collin?" he asks.

"What could it hurt at this point?" I ask.

"I really don't think you should, Steph."

"I want to know what happened, Steve."

He quiets and then reaches for me. I stiffen as he pulls me into an embrace.

"All we need to know is that you're alright, we've made it back to land, and we're on our way to Los Angeles. And I'll take care of the rest. I'm going to confront him about the embezzlement," Steve says. "He'll be out of our lives in a matter of days."

I know that's not true, though.

Any court proceedings could drag on. And there's no telling how Collin will react to Steve confronting him. Especially if the way Collin reacted to me was to push me off the boat, hoping that I wouldn't come out of the water alive.

"I think the police should be there when you confront him," I say.

"I'll take care of it, Steph," he tells me.

I don't like the way he says it, implying that he might not call the police.

"Fine," I say. "But I'm going on the retreat tomorrow night."

He furrows his brows and takes a deep breath.

"I really don't think you should," he says firmly.

"I'm going to," I say with resolve.

Steve takes another breath, steeling himself. It's like he's trying not to get angry.

I step back a little, putting distance between us, but he immediately reaches for my wrist and tugs me back.

"I don't want us to be upset with each other. We need to stick together," he says.

There's a sadness in his voice. The irritation is gone. I relax into his embrace.

"We will," I say. "You'll be right there with me the whole time," I assure him. "The worst thing that could happen is that I have a bad trip and don't remember anything at all. It's basically a shot in the dark," I say.

He nods, though the expression on his face makes me think he's less than sure.

"It'll be okay," I say. "And it might even help."

He sighs and gives me a sad smile.

"You've always been one of a kind," he says. "I've never been able to tell you anything," he says. "And that's one of the things I love about you."

There's something wistful in his eyes. Like he's thinking about the past, just like I have for the last few days.

I smile at him.

"I love you so much," I say. "I will always love you."

"I will always love you, too, Steph," he says.

And then he pulls me into a tight embrace.

TWENTY-FOUR

WHEN WE DISEMBARK from the boat, I feel immense peace as solid ground meets the soles of my feet. I breathe a deep sigh of relief. Even though we're hardly back in Los Angeles yet, this feels like a huge step in the right direction. Luggage rolling behind me, we all head for the taxis that have been ordered to pick us up at the dock.

The ride to Iquitos takes only a few minutes as the city butts up right against the Amazon River. I look out the open window of the little bus we find ourselves on and take in the sights. Hotels dot the landscape along with the living arrangements of locals. People smile and laugh in the streets and others look serious, dead set on a mission as they walk down the road.

Feeling less isolated brings almost immediate relief.

If anything were to happen here, there would be people to witness it.

And I can't get over how nice it feels to be back on solid ground.

We arrive at the hotel we're staying in for the next two days. It's quaint, with a cursive neon sign declaring its name: The Anaconda Inn. I'm sure it's the most used by tourists with its English name and the over-the-top decor in the lobby. Gilded vases with peacock feathers in them greet us on either side of the check-in desk.

Steve checks us in, and then Collin does the same for him and Cece.

"Meet in the lobby at 7?" he asks before they disappear into the elevator. Their room is on the second floor and ours is on the first. I'm grateful for the extra separation.

"Sure," Steve says, though there's still some doubt in his voice. Like maybe he hopes I'm going to change my mind.

I feel bad for him. I know he's worried, and I also know that I'm not changing my mind.

At all.

I'm doing this, because there's a chance that it will work.

"See you then," Collin says, looking at me but speaking to Steve. It sends a chill up my arms despite the heat wafting in from the street.

After they disappear into the elevator, I turn to Steve.

"Come on," I say, leading us down the hallway that leads to the rooms on the first floor.

He follows without a word, seemingly resigned to the fate I've assigned him. He unlocks the door and lets us into the room. It's humid despite the air conditioner. There's a tube TV that's outdated by about twenty-five years. The walls are bare and there's a Bible and a telephone on the single nightstand next to the queen bed.

"Being overnight in the jungle will be preferable," I joke, trying to get Steve to laugh.

He smiles a little, a chuckle escaping him.

"You really have no idea what it means to 'rough it,' do you?" he teases. "How are you going to make it in the jungle for a night?"

"I looked up the retreat. You get to stay inside a hut with screened walls. All the atmosphere of the jungle without the bugs," I say with a smile.

"If you say so," Steve says with a good-natured shrug.

"It'll be fine," I tell him, trying to sound as sure as I can.

There's a tiny little niggling doubt in the back of my mind. Steve is right, this could go wrong. And even though I assured him the worst thing that could happen would be a bad trip, I'm not sure *how* bad that could be.

Would my head injury impact that?

What if my mind goes somewhere I don't want it to?

It's a little frightening. But I'm sure these are probably the normal concerns people have about an experience like this.

Right?

AT SEVEN, we meet Collin and Cece in the lobby. Collin's already called a taxi, and it's waiting for us outside as the sun is hanging lower in the sky, getting ready to dip below the horizon. Soon, we'll be at an isolated hut in the woods with a stranger guiding us through a psychedelic trip.

The reality of the situation starts to sink in.

This could be dangerous. I have no idea how my mind will react to such a substance. I remind myself that it's temporary. In the morning, it will be over, and there's a tremendous amount I stand to gain.

Steve squeezes up next to me in the cabin.

"You're quiet," he whispers to me.

I nod and smile at him, wondering if he knows what I'm thinking. That I'm wondering if maybe he's right. That we should just stay at the hotel. But before long, we're moving away from the hotel and the inertia of the evening takes over. We pass through the streets and soon we're on the outskirts of town, driving over a bridge toward the rural area on the opposite side of an offshoot of the Amazon.

We head into the jungle on a small dirt road that leads to the retreat. It's darker in the jungle, the sun obscured by the tree canopy, and as the moments pass, it gets less and less light around us. The sun is beginning to set. We drive for almost forty-five minutes, deeper and deeper into the wild. At that point, it occurs to me that there's no turning back. We're committed now.

"You okay?" Steve asks, squeezing my hand.

The rattle of the frame of the van against the dirt road is loud enough that our companions don't hear our conversation.

"I'm fine," I tell him, maybe more for my own sake than his.

The driver takes a turn onto an even less-traveled road and soon, we're sitting outside of what looks like a tiny visitor's center. It surprises me how commercialized it looks, all the way out here in the jungle.

"Here you go," the driver says as he parks. He hops out and opens the back door for us to pour out. Steve and I are last, our seats at the very back of the van. Once we get out in front of the center, I see the sign.

Ancient Knowledge Retreat Center

A nice euphemism for *a good place for privileged white tourists to do drugs that aren't legal in their own country, all while disguising it as a cultural learning experience.*

I feel a twinge of guilt at being here.

A tan man with a long black ponytail comes out of the entrance to the center and throws his arms wide, welcoming us to this little oasis in the jungle. He opens his mouth to say something, and just then, the little van sputters off, back toward the main road, making it impossible to hear him.

"Sorry," he says, clearing his throat as the rumble of the vehicle grows more distant. "I'm Juan Miguel and I'll be your guide for the night."

His accent is faint, and his dress is flamboyant. A long, multicolored poncho hangs over his body. He looks to be in his thirties or forties.

"I own the center," he goes on. "You'll be taking

ayahuasca tonight with the help of my grandfather, who is a local shaman."

There's something about the whole thing that strikes me as far too *packaged*. Like it's been tailor made to fool tourists into thinking they're having an authentic ancient Peruvian experience. It doesn't sit right with me. I cross my arms as we listen.

"So, everyone come inside. We have clothes for you to change into, something more comfortable. And then we will go out to the hut and get started."

He smiles at all of us.

Collin smiles at Cece, but she doesn't return it. He turns his focus to me and gives me a wink.

Somehow, it makes me feel vulnerable. A gentle reminder that I don't want to be alone with Collin. God, I hope tonight is fruitful. I swallow hard and we follow him into the center.

The place is built of unfinished wood and smells like it, too. On the wall are art prints depicting the ayahuasca leaves and roots. There are infographics about psyche-delics and their benefits, none of which comes with any real medical citation. The place strikes me as somewhere that suburban American couples come after they've had an *awakening* at a spirit fair in the States.

"Here are your clothes. Oversized linen pants and an oversized shirt. All of them should be comfortable. You're going to be spending the night lying on cushions in the hut, so we want you to be in the most comfortable mater-ial. If you're satisfied with what you've worn, you don't have to change. But I would encourage you to do so. The less restricting items you have on your body, such as underwear or socks, the better your experience may be."

"Do you want us to take off our shoes?" Cece asks.

"There are sandals beneath the clothes that you can wear and then you can take them off at the hut," Juan Miguel says with a smile. "I'll be back in a few moments to brief you all."

I reach for the stack of clothing and Steve does the same.

"I should have worn leggings and a t-shirt," I whisper to him. Instead, I'm in a button-up blouse and jeans.

"You and me both," he teases.

The four of us take turns using the single bathroom to change. When Steve disappears inside, I hang close to the door, not wanting to be without him for long.

"Are you excited?" Collin asks, sneaking up on me. I jump.

"Very," I tell him with a smile.

"I hope you have a good trip," he says. Then he reaches up and brushes a hair out of my face. I stand there, shocked into stillness. I don't move, feeling like a baby deer must when a big cat has it pinned to the ground. I'm terrified.

Just as quickly as he invaded my personal space, the bathroom door opens and Steve comes out. Collin steps backward, putting an appropriate distance between the two of us. Steve glances at him, mentally measuring the movement. Then he looks at me as if to ask if there's been a problem. I shake my head, not wanting him to get into it with Collin. Not here. Not now.

Steve's body language seems to relax slightly, taking a cue from me.

Collin smiles at the pair of us and steps back over to his wife.

Just then, Juan Miguel comes back in.

"If you're all ready for the trip of a lifetime, follow me."

TWENTY-FIVE

A NIGHT CHORUS OF BUGS, birds, and monkeys greet us when we come out of the visitor's center. The path is dimly lit with torches, fire casting our shadows long across the dirt path that leads to the hut.

It seems like we walk forever, and I feel butterflies gathering in my stomach. They're unpleasant, though. Perhaps moths instead. Or maybe fruit flies, freshly set on a carcass. The thought turns my stomach and I breathe deeply, trying to still my thoughts. The last thing I need is to go into this with those sorts of thoughts in my head.

Juan Miguel leads us, and finally, up ahead, I see a hut. It's just as I imagined it. Octagonal with wood framing. Large walls made only of two-by-fours and mesh to keep the bugs out. You're out in the elements, ready to commune with nature minus insects that might be carrying diseases.

All the wonder of the ancient world with the amenities of the modern one.

It's just another piece of the puzzle that makes the whole thing feel manufactured. Except for the fact that if you need to use the bathroom out here, Juan Miguel suggests you just step a few feet into the jungle.

He opens the screen door, and it creaks on its hinges. Inside, a fire is roaring in front of what almost looks like a throne. And atop it sits an old man with some of the same facial features that Juan Miguel has. This must be his grandfather, the shaman.

He doesn't look at us as we come in, and only stares at the fire, like he can make out shapes in it. Like it's telling him about the future. It's a little disconcerting, making me think we've caught him at a bad moment. Part of me wants to excuse myself and tell him I'll come back another time.

But I know there is no other time. This is it.

This is an opportunity I wouldn't get so easily back home.

And there's every chance this might work.

I glance at Steve to gauge his reaction to the scene before us.

He looks at me, but his face is unreadable. He says nothing.

"Sit, please," Juan Miguel says.

There are four sets of cushions. I take mine on the farthest right and Steve sits beside me. Collin ends up on the outside left and I'm pleased with the arrangement.

"Now, before we get started, let me give you a little briefing," Juan Miguel says, taking a seat next to his grandfather. An altar extends from either side of the fire, one arm going out in front of Cece and Collin, the other going out in front of Steve and me. On it, there are two empty cups on either side. Juan Miguel goes on. "Ayahuasca can be a life-altering experience. It is common that you should find yourself amongst the stars and able to speak to the god of your choosing. The secrets of the universe become clear, and you become one with it, as you always have been. It's transformative and mind-bending. No one comes away from here untouched. No one comes away from here unaltered by this experience," he says.

The four of us are so quiet before him that the night sounds of the jungle seem to roar around us. He speaks again.

"Do not go into this experience with fear," he says. "That can lead you to a bad place. Go into it with an intention, a positive one, and follow through on it with your journey into the cosmos."

My heart beats faster. I try to convince myself that I feel no fear. But at the core of my being, I know that's untrue. I absolutely feel fear.

I'm terrified of what I might find in my memory.

I'm scared of confronting the awful truth of the moment I was shoved overboard. I almost died, and here I am asking a psychedelic plant to help me conjure the truth about that moment. It's insane. This is *not* a good idea.

There's a part of me that knows I can get up at any moment and call it off. What's stopping me?

But there's another part of me that's committed.

Another part of me wants to see this through. That wants to know what lurks on the other side of my consciousness. That uneasy feeling I've had for the last several days dares me to pick at it.

And in that moment, I know I'm going through with it.

Not because I want to.

But because I can't live with the idea of *not* going through with it.

I take a deep breath and let it out slowly. For a second, the sound of my own breathing seems so loud that I'm self-conscious. I glance at Steve, but he's looking forward to Juan Miguel and his grandfather.

"Is everyone ready?" he asks.

I nod my head along with my companions. And without further ado, Juan Miguel begins the task of making tea with the leaves and roots of the ayahuasca plant.

I watch intently, willing the water to boil as he hangs a pot over the roaring fire. The heat from it has brought a sheen of sweat to my forehead and I swipe at it with my sleeve. Suddenly, the outfit they gave us feels too warm, and I wonder if it's just my nerves. Probably.

Juan Miguel waits until the pot is boiling, and he adds the ingredients. I watch as he puts each one in and then lets them all boil together for a while. I'm not sure how long passes. Minutes? An hour? More? I'm lost in thought and the visual of the pot boiling above the fire is hypnotic, even without any psychedelic effect yet.

Finally, he pulls the pot from the fire and lets the tea

steep. Again, time passes and I'm not sure how long. All I know is that it's fully dark outside now and the fire is practically blinding in the darkness that surrounds us.

Juan Miguel pours the tea into each of the four cups and then he distributes them one at a time, saying a blessing over each of us. When I take my tea, the heat warms my palms. Juan Miguel says his blessing, making a cross in front of my face in the air. It surprises me, the Christian gesture, making me think that Juan Miguel doesn't spend all his time in the jungle with his grandfather. It's a thought that makes me uneasy again, but I remind myself that I've already made up my mind.

I'm going through with this.

We all hold our cups out, waiting for his instruction. He returns to his seat next to his grandfather behind the altar. His grandfather stands and says some words in what sounds like an ancient language. He gestures with his arms and points to each of us in turn. And then he says, in perfect English, "Drink."

He raises his palms in the air, gesturing for us to follow his command, and we do.

I bring the cup of tea to my lips and the smell is nothing remarkable. It smells like earth and when I taste it, it's very bitter. There are notes of earth within the tea and I make a face as I swallow. It seems innocuous enough as I drain the cup, grimacing at the flavor. It's hard to imagine that something so simple is going to take us all far away from this space before the end of the night.

I place the cup in front of me on the altar and sit back on my cushion.

"Lie down," Juan Miguel's grandfather says, pressing his palms down on the air, indicating the movement. And we all obey again, laying back on our sets of cushions.

I stare up at the ceiling of the hut. I wonder what's coming.

I wonder if I've made the right choice.

In the darkness, Steve's hand finds mine and he squeezes.

I turn to look at him and notice how black his eyes seem. I wonder if it's because they're dilated due to darkness or due to the concoction we just drank. Or maybe it's my own imagination, the tea starting to take effect on me. He smiles, squeezing my hand again, and then he releases it.

I feel the grass beneath my fingers as he drops my hand. I touch the ground.

And then we wait.

TWENTY-SIX

I HAVE no idea how much time passes before I begin to see fractals.

Slowly, my vision becomes kaleidoscopic. The fractals move outward infinitely, their centers growing larger and larger and remaining unchanged at the same time. And for a moment, I don't even realize that the drug has begun to take effect.

They dance across the ceiling, growing more colorful. Pinks and pastel purples, bright neons and glitter accompany them. Then they seem to melt into the ceiling of the hut. I blink my eyes several times, hoping that if I open and close them enough, the vision will settle down and go away.

I close my eyes again, scrunching my face up, and roll my head to the side. I look at Steve.

The profile of his body seems to undulate. Like the shape of him is vibrating, changing by the instant. It's minute, but his profile is fluid. When I breathe out, it shimmers, changed by my very breath. When I breathe in, part of him pulls toward me. The vision is at once disconcerting and calming.

We've reached the point of no return, I realize.

And then I'm overcome with a sudden cramp in my stomach. Nausea accompanies it. I clutch my abdomen and roll onto my side.

Just then, I hear the door to the hut open, creaking on its hinges and slamming shut. The sound of footsteps hurrying across the grass toward the jungle.

"Don't go too far," Juan Miguel advises in the distance.

And then I hear the sound of retching.

Someone is vomiting.

And no sooner have I had the thought than I realize I'm next.

I stand, disoriented for a moment. I see the door and make a beeline for it. Juan Miguel opens it for me and gives me the same advice he gave to the person who threw up before me. I race toward the darkness, seeking privacy. And before I can find it, I vomit. And as I throw up, I realize that I'm losing control of my bowels as well. I pull my pants down and squat at the edge of the jungle.

After the worst diarrhea and vomiting bout that I've had since a severe case of food poisoning, I return to the hut, my body feeling annihilated but the high not abating. The world seems even more fluid when I return.

When I get back inside the hut, only one person is seated on their cushion. Cece.

She's got her head hanging between her knees. I

wonder if she's already thrown up or if she's about to. She doesn't bother to respond to the sound of me returning. I find my cushion and sit down, slowly lying back down. I stare at the ceiling again.

The fractals return, but now they begin morphing into other shapes. Things, people, animals. And then the roof of the hut is gone and I'm in the stars. I'm no longer in my body, and the realization makes me momentarily panic.

I breathe intentionally, refusing to give up on this.

I'm not going to have a bad trip.

I repeat the mantra to myself.

I'm going to remember everything.

I repeat this to myself, too.

My heart rate slows, and I calm down as the stars seem to dance around me. I feel my body now and I reach out to touch the ground beside me. I run my fingers through the grass on either side of me and then I open my eyes and look to my right.

A giant tarantula crawls across the back of my hand and I jerk my hand away, sitting up straight. But as soon as I do, the tarantula is gone. A figment of my imagination.

I stare at the spot where it was only a second ago.

I turn, looking over at my companions. Everyone is lying down. Steve has an arm thrown across his face. I wonder if he's having an equally rough experience. But the thought is gone as soon as it forms, replaced by other things that seem to fill my vision.

I look over at the side of the hut again, making sure there aren't any tarantulas.

My eyes drift to the altar, to the fire. And I catch Juan Miguel's gaze. He smiles at me, showing his teeth, and I swear he has fangs.

Transfixed, I stare at him until his grin fades.

In that moment, I feel no self-consciousness. I just want to make sense of what I'm seeing.

I lay back down, eyes open, and stare at the ceiling again. I glance to my side, but the tarantula isn't there. Even so, I cross my arms over my chest in some protective gesture, lying there like a vampire.

I scrunch up my face and will myself to sober up. But just as I do, I feel myself untethering. It's a new sensation. Things feel like they're unraveling. Like the seams of the universe are coming apart and I feel more and more separate from myself.

My mind wanders. I think about the last few days. About going overboard on the boat.

I probe the depths of my subconscious, willing myself to come up with something—the truth. I want to remember and I *need* to remember.

I force myself to breathe, reminding myself that I need to relax. We're safe here. In the morning, this will be a memory. Relax. *In. Out. In. Out.*

My breathing begins to slow.

My memories become more tangible. I imagine them as bits in a stew and I'm fishing with a ladle into the broth for each of them. The first I pull up is the sensation of my head hitting the side of the boat. Such a loud noise it made. A thudding that didn't immediately register with my brain as pain. It took a second.

Then comes the sensation of scales against my leg.

Instead of the murkiness of the water, I see the snake. It turns to face me under the water. It hisses and I can hear it. And then it speaks, its words heavy with *s*.

You know what happened.

You know exactly *what happened.*

I stare at the snake, and it stares at me.

What happened?

The snake laughs.

Exactly what had to.

It turns and swims away and my eyes shoot open. Fractals fill them and I reach up to rub them. Like the motion can remove the fractals from my vision. It doesn't and I close my eyes tightly, willing them to go away.

The next sensation I feel is the thump of being deposited onto the deck of the boat.

Someone cradles my head behind me. My body is limp, unmoving. I'm about to die, I realize.

And then I gasp for air, choking up water.

The burning in my lungs comes back to me. The intensity of the burn of water inside me, restricting my breath. I cough, and cough, and cough until I'm sure I taste blood.

And then I look up and see Steve.

There's a button missing on his shirt.

The button that I found in Collin and Cece's room.

I reach for him, but my arm doesn't move. And before I know it, I'm traveling via stretcher below deck. Fear takes over. The memory of two hands on my back comes to me. *I was shoved.*

By who?

I feel the hands on my back, clear as day. The rainforest lies before me and the River below me. I pitch over the railing. And just before my head hits the deck, I see a face peering over the balcony.

The face of the person that pushed me.

It's Cece.

TWENTY-SEVEN

MY EYES SHOOT OPEN. And in that moment, I'm completely conscious of how quiet it is.

The jungle animals, birds, insects, and the roaring fire are the only sounds that fill the space. Everyone is silent, lying on their backs. Sweat is pouring from my forehead, and I don't move.

Cece.

My vision is clouded with shapes and colors, all of them moving. The surrounding hut seems to be breathing, and suddenly I can hear it.

Inhale. Exhale. Inhale. Exhale.

The whole place groans with life. I need to get out of here. I have to leave.

It's not safe.

I shoot up and scramble off my cushion. I run for the door and grab the handle.

"Stephanie!" I hear Steve's voice behind me.

The door slams and I'm outside. I run for cover, not

daring to look back. Everything seems to be collapsing in on me.

Cece.

Why Cece?

I think of the numbers on the spreadsheet. The amounts that had been transferred into a company bank account in my name. The most familiar number.

1212.

I see hands typing on a keyboard. They're mine. A click of a mouse. I'm searching for something weeks before we left. Am I booking the flight to Peru? Booking the cruise?

My mouse cursor hovers over a button that will allow me to make a purchase.

I run deeper into the jungle.

I see the total.

$1212.

What the hell was it?

My breathing becomes ragged. I hear the door of the hut slam shut. Once, then twice. I hear voices and footsteps. I beat my way deeper into the foliage to hide. I need to hide. They're going to kill me.

Cece is going to kill me. Collin will help her.

They know I know about the money.

They know getting back to Los Angeles will mean police involvement.

They've realized I remember.

The thoughts broadcast out of my mind and I see the radio waves traveling through the dark rainforest. They bounce off of trees and travel further out. I have to keep running.

I trip over vines and my sandals come off when I hit the dirt face first. Grunting, I pull myself upright. I keep going, not daring to slow down enough to grab the shoes. My feet slip on mud and rocks and I claw at a nearby tree to pull myself up. I run again, sharp things, leaves and roots underfoot. I pray I don't fall again.

"Stephanie!" I hear Collin's voice this time. I sprint.

It seems closer than Steve's did a moment ago. Where is Steve?

We need to get out of here. We need safety. We need to be away from them.

My heart races as I run deeper into the jungle. The wildlife quiets as I crash through the greenery and I hear the sound of birds and monkeys scattering as I come.

In the darkness, the fractals return. A heightened awareness of my body comes to me. It's like I can feel each individual cell in my body, and at the same time, I'm no longer a part of it. I'm part of the universe.

This intense knowing that there's something more comes over me, and a moment later it's replaced by the most concrete knowledge that we're all just stardust floating through space and there is nothing else. I feel panic begin to swell in my chest.

I stop running and spin, finding myself in a clearing.

My eyes search the darkness. Little lines follow my vision, leaving pastel and neon trails behind along the places where my eyes just rested. The fractals keep coming, like an overlay on top of the rainforest around me.

The vision of Cece returns. She stands, looking over the edge.

I couldn't have seen her for more than a split second before I hit my head and went under. But I'm confident that I *did* see her that night.

Voices start to come from all around me.

Hers.

My own.

Steve's.

Collin's.

A vision of clawing hands, reaching for my face. I swat them away, telling Cece she's nuts, but I know she's not. I back up, edging closer to the balcony. Steve reaches for her, grabbing her around the waist. He tells her to calm down.

She digs her nails into his forearm, and he lets go.

She's on me again, shouting and doing her best to gouge my eyes out.

He comes to my rescue, pulling her off again. She reaches for his shirt.

She tears away the top button, clutching it in her hand. His shirt hangs open as they struggle. I can imagine her realizing she's holding it later and placing it on the edge of the sink.

"You're a fucking sociopath!" Cece spits at me. Her eyes are bloodshot. She's been crying. "I'll fucking kill you!"

Steve clamps a hand over her mouth and whispers

something to her. She still fights him like a tiger. I back up until I hit the balcony.

I spin, instinctively looking for a way out. And I've no more than turned around when I feel her hands against my upper back, shoving harder than I give her any credit for being able to. It's enough. I'm tall enough that the balcony hits right at my hips, a perfect fulcrum.

And then I'm tumbling down.

I see her face peering over the balcony.

And right as I go under, another face joins her.

Steve.

I scream into the night air. The surrounding jungle reverberates with the sound and all the animals that had been so noisy suddenly go silent. I'm left only with the sound of my own sobbing and my own ragged breath.

"Stephanie!" I hear Steve call out in the jungle.

I realize I'm lost. That my best bet is to reconnect with him. For us to get out of here somehow.

"Steve!" I shout.

I hear movement in the trees around me. Another monkey, scurrying to safety amid the great raucous we're making. First, it's to my left, then behind me, then it's on my right. Then it stops.

And suddenly I'm not so sure it's a monkey at all.

I think of the other afternoon in the jungle. The way the jaguar looked at me. The way it flicked its tail.

Had it been nighttime—like it is now—I wouldn't have stood a chance.

My breathing grows shallower, and I feel this discon-nect from the moment. Maybe it's the terror. Maybe it's the realization I've just had about the people I'm with. Our situation. The fact that Steve and I should never have come here.

It's at this moment, I realize I'm crying. Audibly.

"Steph!" Steve calls through the jungle. He's closer now.

"Come, please!" I sob.

I try to gauge if he's closer or further away than he was a few moments ago. And then I hear the snapping of a tree branch and the sway of a limb, leaves brushing against each other. It comes from behind me and I whip around.

The rainforest takes on a glow. All that was dark is dusted with neon and pastel, reminding me of the Lisa Frank posters that my dentist had as I was growing up.

"Who's there?!" I shout.

Whatever is making the noise stops, and the jungle goes silent.

A breeze comes through, cooling my sweaty face, neck, and arms. It's refreshing, a gentle reminder that I have to survive this. There's life to live out there. Steve and I are going to make it back to Los Angeles. All of this will just be a bad memory soon.

No one calls back to me. I hear another bit of movement in the forest. This time it comes from my left, and I spin to face it. Wondering when the noisy visitor will make themselves known. It occurs to me that it could be Cece or Collin, waiting to catch me off guard.

Waiting to finish the job.

"Steve!" I shout.

My voice comes out desperate, echoing around the canopy like the cry of a howler monkey looking for its troupe.

Mine is somewhere else. Somewhere close and yet so far away at the same time.

I begin to cry again, realizing the desperate nature of the situation. I need Steve to find me, but he doesn't call back. I'm met with only the silence of the surrounding jungle and the vague idea that something is stalking me. Something or someone.

And just as those horrible thoughts are catching up with me, I hear the snap of a twig across the clearing. I whirl, and then I see him.

Not my husband.

Collin.

Drenched in sweat and eyes wild with the drug, he steps into the clearing.

And when he sees me, he smiles.

TWENTY-EIGHT

"THERE YOU ARE," he says, his grin widening. "I was worried you'd gotten lost."

"I'm fine," I tell him, feigning confidence.

"Why did you run off back there?" he asks. "Did you remember something?"

He says the last quietly, almost like he's hopeful that I did. I wonder what kind of sick fantasy he's living out right now.

"Just do it," I say.

He furrows his brow in the moonlight.

"What are you talking about?"

He steps closer.

I step back.

"If you're going to get rid of me, just do it already," I spit.

Collin barks out a little laugh.

"Get rid of you?" he asks.

"Stop playing fucking games," I say.

"What games?"

"You lied to me the other day," I say. "You never knew your mother."

He stiffens, standing up straighter, realizing that I've got his number, apparently.

"I'm sorry," he says. "I did it because I thought it was necessary."

"Necessary for what?" I ask him.

"You really don't remember, do you?"

There's a note of something in his voice and I struggle to discern if it's anger at me or frustration with the whole situation.

"I remember that your wife pushed me off that boat," I say with confidence.

"What else do you remember?" he asks.

"Why should I tell you?" I snap.

"I'm not going to hurt you," he assures me, taking another step forward.

I step back and almost stumble over a root of a nearby tree. I struggle to keep my balance and my heart rate skyrockets. For a moment, my mind interpreted it as me being attacked by the jaguar I was sure was out here only moments ago.

Getting my footing, he reaches for my arm and steadies me, helping me stand upright.

"What do you remember, Stephanie?" he asks.

"I told you," I say. "Your wife tried to kill me."

"Why would she do that?" he asks.

"Don't try to gaslight me. I know what I remember. And she had a good reason," I say.

He arches a brow and loosens his grip on my arm. I pull away.

"She knew that I found out about the account you opened in my name," I say. "The company you set up *in my name*. The money you were stealing from us."

Collin stares at me, shock on his features.

Hah!

He didn't count on me remembering *this*.

"Steve knows, too," I say. "And he's on his way here right now."

Collin shakes his head and stoops, putting his palms over his face.

"I risked everything for this," he says with a bitter laugh. "*Everything*."

"Maybe you shouldn't have," I snap.

He looks at me, the two of us standing under the night sky deep in the Peruvian jungle.

"I'm sorry she tried to hurt you," he says. "I truly am."

I laugh.

He cracks a sad smile.

"You really don't believe me," he says, almost to himself.

"Why would I?" I ask.

"I guess you have no reason to," he says with a shrug.

"Steve!" I call out, hoping that my husband will call back, closer than ever before.

"Stephanie!"

His voice booms louder than only a moment ago.

"He's coming," I say.

"Isn't he always?" Collin says with a smirk.

I furrow my brow at him.

I step back, hoping that I miss the root again, but not daring to look away from Collin's face.

Like a bolt of neon lightning, the effects of the ayahuasca hit me in another wave. The neons of the surrounding jungle grow more intense, the glitter trails in my vision more sparkly.

$1212.

I stumble and Collin moves forward, catching me once again and putting me upright.

"What's 1212?" I ask him. "Twelve hundred and twelve dollars. What does that mean?"

With his hands on my arms, his face lights up. His eyes seem to glow in the darkness. I shrink from him and he tightens his grip on me.

"You remember," he says. "It was the cost of the ticket to Cuba."

I stare at him, bewildered.

"Why would you buy a ticket to Cuba?" I ask.

He just laughs.

"What else do you remember, Stephanie?" he asks.

I struggle to form words. The excitement on his face unnerves me. My skin crawls under his gaze.

"You planned a murder?" I ask, putting the pieces together. "The two of you. You were going to kill me, and then him, and then the two of you were going to Cuba?"

He shakes his head with a laugh.

"You're so close."

He pulls me closer to him, close enough that I can

feel his breath fan across my cheeks. The tea and the vomit have made it sour. I smell bile with every word.

"You're so pretty when you're scared," he says.

I recoil at the statement, and the idea that I'm alone with him out here occurs to me.

Jesus Christ, Steve. Get here already.

"Don't pull away," Collin says.

I can't help it, it's instinctive. Feeling the danger the situation holds, I can't do anything *but* pull away from him.

"Please, let go of me," I say.

"Oh, Stephanie," he says. "I'd do *anything* for you, but I'll never let you go."

The phrase rings familiar in my mind. It resonates deep inside of me. And as the memory begins to take shape, I feel the ayahuasca taking root deep inside my mind, driving the truth out. And just as I submit to it, Collin leans forward.

"Nothing will keep us apart," he whispers.

And then he kisses me.

TWENTY-NINE

IT WAS *your favorite thing to say to me.*

I'd do anything for you.

You did whatever you could for me, for the most part. It was just that tricky bit of leaving Cece that seemed to trip you up.

I couldn't really complain, though, seeing as how I couldn't bring myself to tell Steve it was over.

The trip to the Amazon had been my idea. One last hurrah before we made it final. A chance for both of us to see if we really wanted to go through with ending our marriages and starting over.

A large part of me feared that you'd fall back in love with her in the rainforest.

I didn't worry so much about me and Steve.

It had been so long since he'd even noticed me that I wasn't counting on that to happen just because we'd changed our latitude and longitude. I was sure that Steve had lost interest in me a long time ago. When I saw you walk into that cocktail party a couple of years ago, I knew I would be doomed if I were ever alone with you.

And you saw to it that the ball would be set in motion that very night.

I fell in love with you. Hard and fast in the absence of affection from my husband.

There was a guilt about it. The knowledge that this was how my second marriage had started and a third made it a pattern. I'd even shared that with you.

But you were confident that it was fate. Not a pattern.

That there was nothing wrong with either of us.

Even though you were willing to betray both Steve and Cece in order to get what you wanted. Though I can hardly place the blame squarely on your shoulders, because I was willing to put them both through the wringer, too.

And then something happened on the first night of the trip.

I caught Steve staring at me out of the corner of my eye while I was getting ready for our first dinner on board. I did a double take, unsure that I could trust myself. Why would he be looking at me?

I turned and looked at him square on just to make sure.

And he was staring at me in a way he hadn't since he'd stolen me away from Herschel.

"God, you're gorgeous," he'd said.

I was taken aback by the statement, and I laughed a little.

"Don't laugh. It's true," he'd said, and then walked over to me, taking me by the waist and making us both face the full-length mirror on the sliding closet doors. "I don't tell you near enough, but you're the love of my life, Steph."

The words sank into me like the jaws of life, ready to pry open my heart and let everything I'd held away flow right into the core of my being. All the times I'd slept with you and told myself I wasn't in love with Steve anymore. All of that dissipated in that moment, and I was whole again.

"I love you," I'd said.

Tears gathered in my eyes, and I almost told him everything right then and there.

It was in that moment I made up my mind that I was going to end things with you.

Not that night, and not even on this trip, but as soon as we got home.

I was going to close the account we had siphoned money into. Put it all back into Steve's business account. Black Label Trading would be dissolved.

The next night, Cece caught you.

You'd done something so stupid, I couldn't believe it. You'd brought a love letter on the trip with you, tucked into your suitcase. It was in the compartment where you normally stored first aid items. She'd cut her foot on something in the bathroom and didn't want to go downstairs. She got into your suitcase and she found the letter with both our names on it.

And then she went directly to Steve.

Steve had already known. That's why he called the divorce attorneys.

She was so ungodly angry with us. She was more angry at me than at you, something that I've never been able to understand. It was you that should have gone overboard that night, and given the opportunity, I would have shoved you myself, just for being so goddamned stupid.

There was the scuffle in the hallway. And the primary thing I took away from that, other than my head injury and trauma to my brain, was that you never lifted a finger to stop her.

All that time, all those things you'd said to me about how you'd do anything for me, all vanished in a moment. Your cowardice shone through.

Something I should have recognized from the beginning.

Because who has an affair other than a coward?

I should know.

I'd been a coward myself. Too afraid to leave Steve but unwilling to let go of him. Afraid of the pain I might feel in the aftermath. That I might regret things. Never once was I thinking about what the aftermath would be for him. And maybe, just maybe, if I had voiced my concerns about our marriage to him instead of you just once, maybe none of this would have ever come to pass.

On the first night of the trip, I wished I could take it all back. I wanted nothing more than to return to my life, as it was, before I'd met you. I wanted to rekindle my marriage and do anything I could to make it up to Steve that I'd betrayed him.

But then she pushed me overboard. And my memory became a gaping, open wound, and the two of you bled right out of it. You and Cece, just two blanks for etching.

The whole situation became a fresh chalkboard. My memory was washed free of guilt when I hit my head.

It threw a wrench into our plans. I couldn't remember anything about you, Collin.

You were a total stranger to me.

And I think you still are.

Even if I remember everything.

THIRTY

ALL THOSE MEMORIES wash over me. The whole affair. All of it I'd interpreted to be about Steve and me and the way our relationship began. But really, it was about Collin. The way we'd cheated and lied for over a year to get our selfish way. My world implodes.

I pull away from Collin, and the world spins.

I jerk my arm out of his and I fall to the ground, scrambling away from him until my back hits a tree. My feet keep shuffling, because no distance would be enough between the two of us.

What is happening?

We had an affair.

That's why Cece was upset. She found out. She shoved me overboard.

And Steve knew.

He kept it from me.

My mind reels.

Fractals and neon trails obscure my vision. I look up

at Collin and he stands in the middle of it all, the moon behind him with a neon glow. Little trails of light dance around his silhouette and I wonder if he's real. If any of this is real.

God, what I wouldn't give to close my eyes, open them, and be home.

I could wake up in my own bed, all of this a terrible nightmare. What if this is a lucid dream?

The thought fills me with hope. I look down at the ground where little worms are poking their heads out of the earth. It's not real. That wouldn't happen. This is a nightmare.

I laugh and touch one of the worms. When I try to pinch it between my fingertips, it's not there. I feel only my own flesh.

"This is a nightmare," I say to Collin with a triumphant grin. "None of this is happening. I just need to wake up."

A laugh comes out of me, and I sound more hysterical than I ever have in my life.

Just wake up.

Collin stoops to the ground beside me. I recoil from him, willing Steve to hurry up, to find his way through the rainforest and into the clearing. To stop this.

"It's not a nightmare," Collin tells me. "It's happening. And we can still make things right."

I feel relief at his words. The chance to make things right. The chance to turn this all around and go back to our everyday lives. Is he willing to do that?

"We *can* make it right," I tell him.

His eyes light up. Two diamonds in the darkness. It fills me with a dread I wasn't expecting.

"Come on," he says, offering me a hand.

I look at it, his profile still glowing. I look back up at his face. He towers over me. This man that I was willing to ruin my life for. I try to wrap my mind around it. The whole trip, all of it leading up to this moment.

We should have stayed at the hotel.

Steve was right.

I made the worst choice possible.

I'm filled with regret and a sinking feeling. Tucking my knees to my chest, I wrap my arms around them and fold in on myself. I beg some unholy power to stop the effects of the ayahuasca in my system. I just want to go home.

"Come on, Steph," Collin says. "Let's go. There's still time."

I look up at him again, mostly to prove to myself that he's still there.

"This is a dream," I mutter, mostly as a reassurance to myself rather than because it's true.

"It's not," Collin repeats.

I feel a tear on my face that I don't bother swiping at. I let it fall freely and look up at the sky.

Collin's hand is outstretched towards me, and just then, Steve emerges in the clearing.

"Get away from her!" he shouts at Collin.

He rushes him from behind, tackling him to the ground. Collin's body makes a thump when it hits the ground. The sound of the air being forced from his lungs is audible and sickening. I close my eyes when I see blood at his temple.

He scrambles to roll over under Steve, and Steve pins him to the ground, then slaps the shit out of him. Steve stands.

"Stay down," he tells Collin in the meanest voice I've ever heard my husband use. He backs up and wipes his forehead. There's blood on his hand. He paces back and forth for a moment, then turns his attention to me. "Are you alright?" he barks in the same tone.

I only nod my head, afraid to speak.

This can't be real.

Steve keeps an eye on Collin as he approaches me. His tone softens considerably.

"Are you alright?" he asks, kneeling in front of me.

I glance at Collin, making sure he's not moving.

I nod my head frantically, and he helps me stand. I cling to him when I get up, not wanting to let go until we're back in Los Angeles.

"Let's go," I insist.

Steve takes a moment to look me over, making sure that I'm in one piece. Satisfied, he nods.

"He lied to you, Steph," Collin says tauntingly from the ground.

We both look at him.

"Shut up," Steve says.

I think about what Collin told me. My mind is vulnerable, my defenses down. I turn to my husband.

"Why didn't you tell me she pushed me?" I ask. "Why didn't you tell me you were angry?"

My voice breaks.

Steve looks at me and, even in the moonlight, I can read the pain on his face.

His breathing is still heavy from fighting with Collin. He looks down, defeated, and then looks back up at me.

"I didn't want you to remember," he says. "The affair."

I stare at him, trying to make sense of what's happening.

"When you were in the infirmary, I realized you didn't remember. Or at least I had that thought. As time went on, it became clear you didn't remember the affair. And things felt like they had. It felt like the early days. I struggled with the idea of telling you. Whether it was the right thing, I couldn't bring myself to do it," he says.

He hangs his head. I step toward him and reach for him, taking his hand.

"You did the right thing," I tell him. "I'm so sorry."

I choke out a sob.

"I'm the one that should be apologizing."

"I'm just glad you're alive," Steve says.

I stand there, taking in the surreal nature of what's happening. Part of me thinks it's just the ayahuasca. In a moment, I'll open my eyes and I'll still be lying inside the hut. Maybe none of this is real.

I hope none of this is real.

"We can just go back to how things were," Steve says.

Collin laughs on the forest floor.

We both look at him.

"Shut up," Steve spits.

"You'll never be able to go back to the way it was before," Collin says with a degree of arrogant joy in his voice.

"Maybe you won't," I say, my voice sounding shrill.

"Of course I won't," Collin says with another laugh. "I risked everything for you. You know that, don't you?"

"I changed my mind," I tell him. "Quite literally."

He laughs again and I fight the urge to grab a handful of earth and shove it down his throat so he never makes that awful sound again.

"Stop," I say instead. My voice comes out as a croak.

I want nothing more than to disappear. To evaporate out of this moment and back into my real life. Back into the life I was leading before any of these horrible things ever happened.

"Maybe you're being punished," Collin says, still lying on his back. "Maybe this is what we both get."

"Stop," I say, more firmly this time.

It's a thought that's already occurred to me on my own.

The idea that all of this is some kind of retribution from the gods for what the two of us had done together, and all that we were planning after this trip. It would be fitting. To make me fall in love with my husband all over again, only to have it revealed to me that I was betraying him in secret for over a year.

And now I have to live with that.

I don't want to hear it from Collin, though.

"Let's go," Steve says.

I nod, but then I glance at Collin.

"What are we going to do?" I ask.

"Get back to Los Angeles," Steve says firmly. "And then I'll sort this whole mess out."

"What are you going to do, Steve?" Collin asks. "Call the police?"

Steve's nostrils flare in anger.

"You can't," Collin says simply. "Because your wife's name is on that account. She stole money from you."

"I'll tell them I gave it to her," Steve bites down on each word. This is killing him. It brings tears to my eyes.

I never meant to be this person.

"Let's go," I tell Steve, turning my focus back to him and imploring him not to stay here with Collin. We need to get moving. A wave of the ayahuasca hits me, making me woozy. The treetops are breathing, I realize. Expanding outward and contracting inward in sync with my own breathing.

I stare at them for a moment, marveling at it.

I look back at Steve, and he glows. Maybe it's the surge of emotion I feel for him, but he looks more handsome than he ever has. I grab his hand and squeeze it, pulling his attention back to me.

"We can never go back to the way things were, Steph," Collin says in an almost sing-song tone. "It's too late for that."

I don't want to listen to anything else he has to say.

I'm ready to get the hell out of here. I look at Steve and nod.

"Let's go," I say.

He nods at me, and then leads me across the clearing and into the jungle once more.

THIRTY-ONE

AS WE START CUTTING our way through the jungle, Steve tries to orient us by the stars each time we come to an area with any clearing in the canopy. He looks up and I wonder how he's able to tell anything. The stars seem infinite out here. There are so many of them, and by my drug-addled estimation, they seem to be moving.

Steve seems unfazed and keeps walking, silently turning us a degree or two at different points.

"I know it's this way," he mutters to himself.

Treading over roots and vines on my bare feet, I start to realize how sore they are, and that I might have cut my right foot at some point when I was running terrified into the rainforest. We stop at another moonlit clearing and I bend over, balancing on one foot so I can rest the other on my knee and look at it.

"Shit," I say.

"Did you hurt yourself?" Steve asks.

"Yeah," I tell him.

The blood seems to glow, and its edges undulate. I'm lucky that the experience I'm having isn't more powerful. But I also realize my brain has gone into survival mode. I'm willing to suffer through anything if it means I'll live at this point.

Just then, both of us hear something. The sound of something traveling through the jungle. Fast movement and then an abrupt silence. The monkeys, birds, and insects go quiet in an instant.

I feel the hair on the back of my neck stand up.

It's that same feeling I had just before Collin emerged into the clearing.

And this time I'm not sure what's scarier: him or a jaguar.

I stiffen and dare to turn my head, looking at my husband.

Steve is still, slowly scanning the trees around us. I do the same, looking for any indication of a threat, but I come up empty-handed.

"Did you hear that?" Steve whispers after a moment.

It feels like an eternity. What I wouldn't give to be back on that stupid boat.

"Yes," I hiss.

Suddenly, there's another rustling of leaves. Then an abrupt stop.

I spin around, unable to keep myself from moving quickly. Death, it seems, is at our door. Moving fast might be my last resort, not that it'll do any good against a three-hundred pound cat with ultra night vision.

I just want to be home.

The thought brings an unexpected tear to my eye.

A realization begins to dawn on me. I think about all the turns we've made and how Steve has adjusted our course. And then I think about him muttering to himself, almost out of frustration. We might be lost, I realize.

The thought fills me with terror. Being lost in the jungle is a horrifying notion.

I think about Tyler telling us we could be ten feet from the trail and never be seen again.

That's what this feels like.

That's what's happening now.

"We need to scream," I say softly.

"What?"

Steve looks at me like I've lost my mind.

"We need to give Juan Miguel an idea of where to look," I whisper.

"You're right," Steve says. But then he hesitates, something seeming to come to the forefront of his mind. I wonder if we're thinking the same thought. "Why—"

"Why haven't we heard him?" I voice the question in an almost normal tone.

We haven't heard them calling for us. I haven't heard Cece calling for us.

What if the jaguar snuck up behind and them and silently broke their necks? No screams. No signs. Pure predator versus unwitting prey in the Amazonian rainforest.

Each thought seems more horrible than the last.

What if we're lost?

What if all our companions are dead?

And what if the people who could get us out of here are dead, too?

I stare at Steve in the darkness, willing the effects of the ayahuasca to settle down, but they seem to come in waves. I take a deep breath, steadying myself.

"It's going to be alright," I say, as much for my benefit as Steve's. "We need to keep going," I tell him, nodding firmly.

He looks at me, eyes wide, and I realize for the first time that he's afraid.

Somehow, that's scarier than any thought I've had thus far.

Steve is not someone who scares easily. He's always been the person I've looked to for protection.

The idea that a situation could be such that he'd be fearful is a soul-crushing notion. I can't let myself think about that. We don't have time to think about things like that.

"Come on," I say. "We have to go."

He nods and begins to lead us through the jungle again.

We walk for what seems like an eternity. I wonder if we're ever going to get out. Minutes turn into half an hour, and that turns into an hour. Finally, I begin to feel a bit of panic.

"Where are we?" I ask him, as if he'll have a clue.

"I have no idea, Steph," he says, his voice resigned.

We stop walking. The surrounding rainforest is alive

with the sounds of the night. I didn't realize how reassuring those sounds were until they were mysteriously gone earlier. It was just like what happened when I was left alone on the trail.

It had to be a jaguar.

I shiver despite the warmth and humidity.

"You alright?" Steve asks, watching me.

"Fine. Just creeped out," I tell him.

"We're going to get out of here, Steph. They're going to find us."

Neither of us have dared voice the idea that there might not be any *they* to come looking. The other awful thought I have is that Collin and Cece will find us, and who knows what will happen then?

"The road from the bridge went north," he says to himself. "Then we went west. The visitor's center was north and west of the bridge. You ran north into the jungle, and I turned east to follow the sound of your voice. You were north of the hut and to the east."

I let him keep working this out.

"We need to find north," he says, turning skyward. "And then we need to head south and east."

I'm not sure his logic is going to get us there with the distance we've already traveled.

"Which way have we been walking?" I ask.

"West," Steve says. "We've gone too far, I think."

I think that much is true. I don't know that Steve's right about where the hut will be, but I'm willing to give it a shot. I have no better ideas.

"Let's go, then," I tell him.

He nods and we take off in the opposite direction, going southeast.

We walk for a good thirty minutes with no sign of man or beast.

And then we come to a clearing.

Steve steps out into the middle of it and looks at the sky. I do the same and marvel at how many stars there are. Once again, I'm struck by the idea that they're moving. God, I want to be done with this.

"How long does the ayahuasca last?" I ask him as I rub my eyes, seeing fractals behind my eyelids again.

"We should be alright in the morning," he says, head still tilted back.

"Do you think we're any closer?" I ask.

He looks over at me and gives me a little smile. I'm not sure if it's meant to be reassuring or not.

"We're going to get there," he says, instead of answering my question. It makes me uneasy, but I follow Steve across the clearing and back into the jungle. It swallows us up into darkness again, and it takes my eyes a moment to adjust.

And then I run directly into him.

"Shit, sorry," I mutter.

Steve says nothing, but remains standing there, stiff as a board.

"Do you see that?" he asks, his voice a whisper.

I step out from behind him and look forward into the darkness.

Just a small amount of moonlight pours in through the canopy. And I do see it.

About five yards ahead of us, two eyes shine in the darkness.

A jaguar.

THIRTY-TWO

"BE STILL," I whisper, my hands on Steve's shoulders, my fingers digging into his flesh.

The eyes don't move, but twice they blink, disappearing into the darkness and then reappearing in the same spot. I stare at them, having this horrible feeling that they'll disappear. Somehow, that would be worse than anything. As long as I can see them, I know where she is.

I can hear Steve breathing. And I hear myself.

We start to breathe in sync.

Shallow breaths, the sound a reminder that we can't just disappear.

And then the eyes are gone.

"Fuck," I whisper, feeling my entire body grow rigid, as if I can tighten my muscles so much that it encases me in a protective shell. My breathing picks up and so does Steve's.

"Be still," he instructs.

I want to scream at the top of my lungs. Everything in me says we should run.

I know he's right.

It's exactly what Tyler said. We need to be still.

What's even more unnerving is the fact that wherever the cat went, it's not making any noise.

I stare, unblinking, into the darkness. I squeeze Steve's shoulder and he reaches back for me, using his body as a shield to protect me however he can.

Fuck. This is terrible.

We just need to make it through the night.

We just need to make it out of here.

There's nothing like multiple brushes with death to make you grateful for your ordinary days.

I'd love to be sitting at home, reading a magazine, and bored out of my mind right now. Christ.

The thought of home is brief. Immediately, I'm brought right back to the moment when Steve speaks.

"We should keep going," he says.

The jungle around us hasn't grown quiet, a pretty clear indication that the cat is gone. My body relaxes slightly.

"Okay," I say with a shaky breath.

Steve goes on, leading us through the dark foliage. As I step barefoot through the rainforest, I wonder what kinds of parasites there might be on the jungle floor. It's a thought that can wait for a later date to be addressed.

A date when we're back in civilization.

I think of the hotel room. How uninviting it had

seemed earlier. Now I'd give anything to be watching local programming on that ancient television.

It's strange what we take for granted. How many ordinary moments would we live all over again if given the chance when we're faced with death?

I don't have time to be philosophical, though.

We have to get out of here.

We crash on through the jungle, and Steve is sure that we're headed the right way. Regardless of whether we're headed in the direction of the hut, eventually, we'll have to emerge. I keep repeating this to myself, as if the jungle doesn't stretch on for hundreds of miles in all the wrong directions. Only one of them will get us back to the hut.

God, please let it be this one.

I take a deep breath, trying to still my nerves.

"I'm sorry I insisted we come out here," I tell Steve as we make our way.

He doesn't bother turning around, just presses forward.

"It's hardly worth fighting about now," he says with a laugh in his voice.

There's a note of falsity to it. I cringe when it comes out. I never should have suggested this was a good idea. If I had it to do over again, I wouldn't. I could have gone on to live my life blissfully unaware of the way I'd hurt my husband because he was gracious enough to let me keep living like that.

But I had insisted.

I hate myself right now.

For all of it. What I did to Steve. What it did to Cece. The fact that I wanted to come out here tonight. I could have gone all my life without remembering those things and probably been better for it.

There's no way the night can get worse.

We keep walking, and the jungle spreads out endlessly. Steve takes every opportunity he gets to check our navigation against the stars. Everything begins to take on a psychedelic quality stronger than before. The rainforest around me glows, getting brighter and brighter and giving me the illusion that I'm seeing heat signatures. Bright pink radiates beside me and I snap my head around, expecting that jaguar to jump out of the brush.

My heart pounds every time it happens, and I become jumpier and jumpier. The situation just gets more and more unreal. Finally, I tell Steve I need a break.

"Can we stop for a minute?" I ask, the sound of my own voice sounding different. I swear I can see the sound waves pulse out into the air in front of me. My eyes follow the visions, and Steve reaches for my arm when he turns.

"Are you okay?" he asks.

"I think it's really starting to hit me," I say. "I need a minute."

"It's starting to hit me, too," Steve admits. He closes his eyes, scrunching them up and blinking rapidly, as if to make sure he's not imagining things. But he is. We both are.

"Do you hear that?" I ask, straining my ears and

wondering how much of what I'm experiencing is in my mind.

Steve listens.

"Nothing," he shakes his head.

"I know," I say.

The jungle has gone silent, and I'm not sure how long it's been that way. Has the cat been stalking us? Following us along the trail and waiting for a moment like this?

I spin around, pressing my back against Steve's.

"Do you see anything?" I ask.

"I don't," he says. But I can hear in his voice that he's not entirely certain he can trust his perceptions.

I feel the same way. It's paralyzing.

What if I'm imagining the silence? What if Steve is imagining it, too? Could he have subconsciously been suggested by me asking if he had heard anything? What if everything is fine?

But what if it's not?

Tears begin to stream down my face. Not because I'm sad, but because I feel everything.

It's too intense, and I choke back my crying.

"It's going to be okay," he assures me.

I want to tell him it's not.

And that it's okay.

And that I'm sorry he's here because of me.

He's going to die, and that's all my fault.

"Steph," he says, his voice soothing. "It's all going to be okay."

The confidence and calmness with which he says it only makes it worse.

"It's all my fault this is happening," I tell him.

"It's not your fault," he says.

"You're too kind," I tell him. "I wish I hadn't brought us out here. I just want to go home."

"We're going to get home," he says.

He says it so surely that I ache for Los Angeles. I imagine us sneaking up beside the Hollywood sign like we did once in the early days of our relationship, after we were married and we didn't have to sneak around anymore.

The thought coaxes a sad laugh out of me.

And then I think I hear a bird chirping.

And another.

A monkey howls.

And insects slowly come back to life.

I heave a deep sigh of relief.

"Let's go," Steve says.

And we start heading through the jungle again.

"It'll be daylight at some point," he says. "We'll be able to get out of here, Steph."

"You're right," I tell him. "I know you're right."

And then I run smack into his back again.

"What is it?" I ask, stepping around him, ready to confront whatever is there.

Steve shuffles his foot against the ground.

"Oh," he says.

The sound is so small, but as soon as I hear it, I know something is very, very wrong.

And when I look down at his feet, I see the linen of a pant leg illuminated by a shard of moonlight. My eye follows it up, over the thigh, past the waist, the torso, the neck, and to the face. I stoop, making sure I'm seeing what I think I am.

I reach out.

"Don't touch her," Steve says, pulling me back.

I stumble onto my backside and sit there, transfixed, in the dirt. A vine is wrapped around her neck, digging in so hard it makes the flesh on either side bulge.

Laying against a tree, vine used as a ligature, there she is.

Cece is dead.

And she's been strangled.

THIRTY-THREE

"OH, MY GOD," I say, bringing my hand to my mouth.

Suddenly, I feel like I'm going to vomit. And then my stomach turns. I throw up right beside myself until there's nothing left. Wiping my mouth, exhausted, I turn back to Cece's body.

The vines move, slithering across her throat like snakes. Like the jungle itself is the culprit. They undulate like serpents, and I swear more come out of the foliage to suck her down into the dirt. I stand quickly, horrified. I brush off my clothes for any trace of her. I don't want to be infected with whatever this is.

I start to swat madly at my arms and my hair. I feel bugs all over me. Spiders everywhere. The vines are crawling up my calves, winding their way up my thighs and I begin to scream.

"Shh!" Steve hushes me, coming to my rescue.

He fights with me, struggling to stop my erratic movements. Finally, he gets me restrained, but I struggle, still feeling the vines crawling up my body.

"I'm going to die," I tell him, gasping for air, already feeling like they're choking me.

"You're having a panic attack," he tells me. "It's okay. Just breathe. Deep breaths. Slow it down."

I stare into his eyes, the only lighthouse I've got in this storm. I can still feel the vines, but I do as he says. Breathe in, breathe out, even though each breath is excruciatingly slow and not getting enough oxygen into my blood. I feel like I'm going to die right here and now.

Slowly, my heart rate seems to be returning to normal. My breathing grows more regulated.

I look down at my legs, but only see the white linen of my pants. I pull them up, inspecting my calves.

"You're okay," Steve says.

I look at Cece, trying to take in the sight before me.

"She's dead," I say, not ready to believe it. But there's one more fact about the scene that's even more disturbing.

The vines around her neck.

The rainforest didn't strangle her.

"He killed her," I say, once again breathless.

I look over at Steve, hoping against hope that he's going to tell me I'm wrong. That's not what happened. That things like this just happen in the jungle. Or maybe that I've hallucinated the whole thing.

I look back at Cece when Steve doesn't respond.

In the darkness, she already looks pale.

Only a few hours ago, she was alive.

Breathing.

Right there beside us in the hut.

I hear Collin's voice, an echo in my mind.

We can never go back to the way things were, Steph. It's too late for that.

He had murdered her before he stumbled into the clearing.

"I think I'm going to have another panic attack," I say softly.

"No," Steve says, stepping up in front of me.

He takes me through the breathing exercise again, and somehow I keep the panic at bay.

"We have to get out of here," he reminds me.

There's only one good thing about the discovery.

We're closer than we were to the hut.

"We're almost there," I tell him.

He nods, as though he's had the same realization. I look back at Cece and marvel at how her dead body has brought a moment of clarity and hope. It reminds me of every survival story I've ever heard. How people would be in these extreme scenarios and have these moments of clarity.

It feels surreal that I could be having that experience right now.

Steve reaches for my hand.

"We just need to get out of the jungle. And we're close," he says.

I nod, wordless.

My gut is knotted with dread. Collin is still out here.

As we begin moving through the rainforest again, I can't shake the feeling that we're being watched.

It's your imagination.

There are a million things that could be giving you that feeling.

You just discovered your murdered friend, for Christ's sake. Of course, you feel that way.

I use the last sentiment to calm myself down. It's the truth. Anyone in the same situation would be unnerved by that development. You'd have to be a psychopath not to be.

Still, the thought that Collin is out there comes back to me.

Maybe Steve injured him enough to slow him down.

Maybe he's still in the clearing.

It wouldn't be in his best interest to come back.

Unless all of us were gone and he could tell any story he wanted.

Another dark thought, that one really chills me.

Did he come out here tonight knowing this would be the outcome?

That he'd kill his wife?

The questions bring on that familiar uneasiness, and I feel the stirrings of an upset stomach again.

"Let's stop again," I say, needing a moment to quell my nausea.

Steve turns and nods, though I can tell by the expression on his face that he'd absolutely rather keep going.

I lean against a tree and will myself better. I force myself to think of something positive. Something that doesn't have to do with anything that will make me sad. I think about how I've always loved those old motel-style keychains. And how they had one on the boat. I hope Steve kept it.

One day, I'll be an old woman, telling this story to someone.

How Steve and I survived our night in the jungle.

The trip of a lifetime.

And at the end of the story, I'll pull out the actual Jaguar keychain for dramatic effect.

The person will take it reverently, examining it like it can't be real. Like the story they've just heard is far too fantastic to be something that *actually* happened. But I'll assure them that it was. I'll tell them they can find a little article in a Peruvian paper.

I see the headline.

Two Americans Survive Psychedelic Trip in Jungle.

Somehow, this thought energizes me.

When I finish telling the story, Steve will swoop in, out of nowhere, like the leading man and plant a kiss on my cheek. The person will look at us like we're magic. Like they've never seen two people so interesting and beautiful.

I smile down at the ground, staring at the roots of the tree I'm leaning on.

"We're going to get out of here, Steve," I tell my husband.

I stand upright, my uneasy stomach gone. I nod at Steve.

"Let's go. No more stopping."

And he nods.

THE VISIONS of the future carry me forward. The ayahuasca intensifies and then lessens, over and over, as we travel. After about thirty minutes, I tell Steve to stop.

"Do you hear that?" I ask.

He stops and still, listening.

"Voices?" He asks.

"In the distance," I say with a laugh. "Oh, my God."

"Hello!" Steve calls out into the night at the top of his lungs.

I laugh, giddy at the prospect of *people*.

A faint *hello* comes from somewhere distant in the direction we've been headed.

"Oh, my God. It's a person," I say.

"Holy shit," Steve says as he grabs me in a rough embrace. He lifts me from the ground and we press our lips together. I taste the bitterness of the tea on his mouth, but I don't care. I love Steve. I always have. And I'll spend forever making this right.

I pull away, thrilled with excitement. We're saved.

But then I hear something behind us. The crackle of foliage.

Oh, my God. It's help!

But when I turn, my stomach drops.

Standing in the middle of the trail, blood dripping from his face and arms, is Collin.

And he smiles wickedly at the pair of us.

I step backwards, and Steve immediately puts himself between the two of us.

"Oh, come on, now," Collin laughs. "We're all good friends, aren't we?"

"Collin," Steve says, sounding like he's reasoning with the devil. "Everything can still be alright. We can tell them that Cece tangled herself in some vines and panicked."

"Oh, that *is* what I'll be telling them. In fact, it's what we planned to tell them, right, Steph?"

I swallow hard, looking over Steve's shoulder at this man I don't recognize.

"You murdered her," I say softly.

"Because you told me to, Steph," Collin spits.

"What?" I bark out a laugh. But I feel a hollowness in my chest.

Collin laughs.

"That was the plan. Run off into the jungle. I'd get rid of her. Then we'd get rid of him together," Collin says, so matter of fact that it feels like I've jumped from a dock in the North Sea.

"You're out of your mind," Steve says.

"Ask her," Collin says. "Look at her face if you don't believe me."

I open my mouth to protest.

Steve glances over his shoulder at me, enough uncertainty that he chances a look at my face.

"He's insane," I say, pointing at Collin.

"Steph," Collin says. "This was always the plan. Why do you think we had those tickets to Cuba?"

1212.

A ticket to Cuba.

Two entries of that same exact number.

"Cuba is unlikely to extradite," Collin says simply. "We were going to take off from here straight to there. Start over."

A seriousness comes over Collin's features.

Steve turns and looks at me, more pain in his eyes than I've ever seen. And also the look of a man that doesn't recognize his wife.

"Is this true?" he asks.

THIRTY-FOUR

THE IDEA CAME *to me right before we left for the trip.*

The ayahuasca retreat. It was the perfect time.

I called you and asked you to meet me behind the abandoned strip mall. I grabbed my keys off the counter as soon as we hung up. Steve was in his study and I called out a goodbye.

"Where are you going?" he asked.

There was no jealousy in his voice, just curiosity. Likely because he wanted to see if I'd get him something while I was out.

"Going to the post office," I said, annoyance in my voice.

"Want to pick up dinner?"

I groaned in the hallway and leaned against the wall. Looking up at the ceiling, I told him I would. I rolled my eyes and shook my head as he told me to pick and surprise him.

I left just after that and headed for the strip mall.

I waited twenty minutes for you to show up. After you parked, you got out of your car and into my SUV.

"Turn off your phone," I told you as I killed the engine of the SUV.

You did just as you were told.

And then I presented a plan to you.

Neither of us was eager for the mess that would ensue with the dissolution of our marriages.

"What if we got them out of the picture?" I asked.

Realization dawned on you.

"Steph," you said, an unhinged delight in your eyes. "What's your plan?"

"On the ayahuasca trip. I'll run out into the jungle and you follow. Make sure they come along, searching for us. You take care of her, and then help me take care of him. We'll have to make it look like an accident. And then get the hell out of there. Fly to Cuba. Start over."

"We could, couldn't we?" you asked, seeming to consider it.

There was a part of me in that moment that wondered if I was going too far—no, knew I was going too far. I didn't see a way back. I'd fallen out of love with Steve and if I ever left him, he'd ruin me. What little we had in the Black Label Trading account wasn't enough to start a life with. I'd be relying on Collin for the rest of the money for that. And if Cece was getting alimony, there was a good chance that Collin and I neither one would be living the lifestyle we'd become accustomed to.

We had sex in the SUV.

Something about the combination of death and sex. I've only known it twice now, but it's intoxicating.

I got Chinese food for Steve, but I didn't eat that night.

The trip was a week away. And I knew that there were still things that could go wrong with our plan. Anything could happen.

And it did.

THIRTY-FIVE

"OH, NO," I whispered.

Every bit of solid ground I'd found with my visions of the future crumbles in an instant.

The memory is solid. It's real.

This *really* happened.

Cece is dead.

And it's because I told Collin to make it so.

"Oh, no. Oh, no. *Oh, no.*"

I crumple to the ground, and the breath is sucked from my lungs as the weight of the truth crashes down over me. Not daring to look Steve in the eye, I cover my own, beginning to rock back and forth, willing this not to be true.

Willing *anything* other than this to be the truth.

"Is that true?" Steve repeats, his voice breaking.

And I sob. I want to tell him it's not, but I know beyond a shadow of a doubt it *is* true.

I scream into the night. So much pent-up rage coming

out in that instant. I get to my feet and charge Collin, shoving him as hard as I can.

He sails backwards, laughing at me. And just as I'm about to throw a punch, Steve grabs my arm.

"Stop!" he shouts.

I slow down and my arm falls. Steve lets go of it, no comfort coming from him.

"There are people looking for us," Steve says, his tone defeated. "I don't care what happens when we get out of here. You can do whatever you want, both of you. I just want to get out of here."

I look at him, and there's a betrayal in his eyes I've never seen.

Not even when we discussed the affair.

Tears stream down my face.

"Don't be mad at me," Collin says, holding his hands up.

I feel rage simmering beneath the surface of my skin, about to make my blood boil. I ball my fists and bite my bottom lip until I taste blood as I stare at him.

"Come on," Steve says, his tone gentler.

It breaks me.

The familiarity of it.

The way he didn't know who I really was.

And the way I betrayed even myself.

I want to die.

Steve stares at Collin, and there's a shift in the energy in the air. It's the most subtle thing, but I feel it intensely. It's like that moment when a dog's body language changes ever so slightly and you know there's about to be a fight.

Before I can act, Steve throws the first punch, hitting Collin squarely across the jaw.

Collin reels from the punch. The smile is wiped off his face in an instant, and I'd be lying if I didn't admit a satisfaction with that.

Steve hits him, over and over, with a force I've never seen him use before.

It's terrifying.

And for a split second, I wonder if this is how he felt when Collin said I wanted to kill him.

Like he was looking at someone capable of violence he couldn't have imagined only moments before.

An affair is one thing.

A murder plot is another.

In the distance, I hear voices calling.

"We're here!" I shout back, willing them to get here in time.

Not for Collin's sake, but for Steve's. I want this nightmare to be over. I want Steve to be okay.

When I turn, Collin has the upper hand, his arm around Steve's throat and a rock in his hand, his arm above his head. He's poised to shatter his skull.

My eyes shoot wide, and I jump forward, throwing my hands up.

"No! Stop!" I scream.

Collin's eyes are wild, the combination of attempting murder and a psychedelic course through his veins. It's all he's thinking about. When I ran out of the hut, he saw that as the green light.

"Please, don't," I beg.

"This is what you wanted, Steph," Collin says through gritted teeth as Steve struggles against him. Collin tightens his arm around Steve's throat as Steve claws for purchase, trying like hell to get some air.

"Please, let him go, Collin," I say.

I make eye contact with Steve.

I know I can't make it right. Whatever we had is shattered eternally.

You can't come back from that.

And I made that choice.

Even still, I can see in Steve's eyes everything that's going through his mind. Every memory he's conjuring, wondering how he couldn't have truly known what kind of person I was.

God, how cruel was the illusion I've been living the last few days.

Thinking that I was a good person. Thinking that I was winning my husband back.

Christ. Did my brain try to protect itself from the truth?

I don't deserve protection from the truth.

I begin to cry. And so does Steve.

"Steph," he struggles to speak.

"Oh, you wanna give her some last words?" Collin taunts. He tightens his grip, choking Steve even more. But then he loosens it. "I guess I can allow that, seeing as how we've all been on quite the roller coaster."

"Steph," Steve says. "Run."

A tear snakes down his cheek and I feel like I've been gutted.

"No," I blubber. "No. I'm not leaving you!"

Collin chokes him harder, and I watch Steve struggle, trying to get a grip that will allow him to alleviate the pressure. His eyes roll in his head, and I scream at Collin.

"STOP!"

"This is what you wanted, bitch!" Collin shouts.

His agitation gives Steve relief for a moment as Collin's grip loosens when his anger turns to me.

"I want my life back!" I shout, my tears making it almost impossible to enunciate the words. It all comes out as a cry. A selfish, entitled cry. The only person that deserves to make such a plea is Steve, and he's telling me to run. "Let him go," I say, getting a hold of myself.

"Too late for that now, honey," Collin says.

And with a swift motion, he brings the jagged rock down onto Steve's skull. There's a sick, wet crunch, and Steve goes limp. Collin lets him collapse and the rock drips with my husband's blood, brain matter clinging to the sharp edge of the rock.

I rush to him, struggling to roll him over onto his back.

I see the hole in his skull. His brain is so pink. So pink.

It glows as I stare at it, and I scream.

I shout his name over and over again, willing him to wake up despite the fatal injury.

"Jesus Christ, stop!" Collin finally shouts. "He's fucking dead, Steph. Just like you wanted."

I sob uncontrollably.

I deserve to be dead. Not Steve.

I look up at Collin through my tears, and he offers me a hand.

I stare at it. The normalcy of the gesture unnerves me and sends me into another crying jag.

"Oh, fuck," Collin groans. "Really?"

"I didn't want this," I blurt.

"You literally asked for this," he says, losing his patience. "You wanted a new life, and I have *given* you that, you ungrateful whore. That's all you are. A whore. I knew that the minute I laid eyes on you. I never wanted this. *You* made this happen."

Collin's words are cruel, and nothing I don't deserve.

"You brought this on yourself, bitch," he spits. "And if you don't get with the program, you're gonna need to go out just like your idiot husband. Don't you get that?" He spins, tapping his forehead, illustrating how stupid he thinks I am.

Fuck. Someone *get* here.

"So, are you on board or not?" Collin asks. "Because I will absolutely kill you if I have to, Stephanie."

"If that's my only option other than to go to Cuba with you, then do it already," I say, my voice monotonous.

He laughs bitterly.

"We went through all of this for you to back out at the most important moment?" he asks.

Collin kneels down beside me.

"Pull it together, baby," he says, brushing a lock of hair out of my sweaty face. "All we have to do is follow those voices and get the fuck out of here. Leave the talking to me. We'll be on our way to Cuba in the morning."

He strokes my face, and I fight the urge to recoil in disgust.

Thinking that I have no other choice if I want to survive, I nod.

He extends his hand again, offering me help to stand.

And I take it.

THIRTY-SIX

I STEEL my nerves and glance down at Steve one last time.

I'll make this right.

Collin pokes me in the back.

"Let's go," he says, pushing me forward into the jungle.

Barefoot, I lead us, following the sound of distant voices.

"What are you going to tell them?" I ask.

I wrack my brain for what can be done. Can I get someone alone and tell them the truth about what happened? Collin will absolutely turn on me and tell them I orchestrated the whole thing, and if he can convince them, I'm sure he'll say I killed Cece myself.

The voices call in the distance and Collin yells back.

The harsh sound of his voice against the quiet of the jungle startles me, and I force myself to keep moving forward.

The fractals return, and so does the neon and pastel glow. The leaves make trails in my vision as I push my way through them. Things seem to glow in the dark. We push onward.

I feel like time has no meaning out here.

I don't know how long passes. But we walk a long time, it seems. And then ahead of me, I see something.

I stop.

"Go," Collin says, pushing me again.

I stumble forward two steps.

In front of us are a pair of glowing eyes.

I can hear the voices of men not too far from us. But those eyes are close. Less than ten feet away, and they stare at me, blinking occasionally. A nasty reminder that they belong to something living. Something that's likely hunting us.

I stare at the cat in the darkness, begging my eyes to make out the shape of it.

"What is it?" Collin asks.

I only point.

He steps up beside me and stills himself, finally growing quiet.

The surrounding jungle is silent. Only the sounds of people calling out to us can be heard.

I swallow, the lump in my throat feeling hard and my mouth dry. The cat's been stalking us all night. It stalked Steve and me some great distance. Has it been hanging back this whole time, watching my progress through the jungle?

Is it going to finish the business it has with me once and for all right now?

I beg it to.

End me.

End all of this suffering.

And then the cat steps out of the darkness, its form taking shape before my eyes.

Fractals radiated outward from it. The cat itself glows pink, its fur teal and purple with black undertones, barely visible in the dark.

My God, it's *gorgeous*.

Suddenly, every myth or folk correlation between the dark feminine and the cat become crystal clear. I imagine societies living in sync with these animals, sharing the same hunting ground. It's no wonder they were revered. As the cat moves, its fur slides over its muscles, each spot gleaming in the darkness.

I stand there, unable to move, staring at the jaguar.

It steps up, about four feet in front of me, and then it sits down right there.

Its tail twitches back and forth and its eyes meet mine.

Two glowing green orbs. The jaguar stares deep into my soul and I feel like in that moment, she and I understand each other. Slowly, I reach out my hand, trembling as it gets closer to the animal. I know this is a mistake.

But the big cat leans forward, pressing its huge head beneath my palm like a pink, purple, and teal house cat of gargantuan size, and I laugh. The sight sends joy spiraling deep into me. The first time I've felt it in ages.

Delight and wonder mingle at the forefront of my soul and I stroke the cat.

I look to my side, and Collin is gone.

I turn back to face the cat, and it still sits there. A loud purring vibrates deep inside it and I see the audio waves traveling through the air. Fractals dance around it and I reach for one of the waves, plucking it out of the air.

It vibrates in my palm, feeling like a cat's throat as you stroke it while it purrs. I marvel at the sensation, staring at the visible sound in my hand.

The cat bats me with a giant paw, drawing my attention back to it.

It steps forward and I kneel in front of it, accepting whatever fate this may be.

I no longer care where Collin went. Or what he's telling the people looking for us.

Any moment now, this cat is going to flip a switch and remember it's a wild animal. Soon after that, my worries will be over. I can die out here with my husband and pay for what I've done when I reach the gates of hell.

I no longer want to find my way back to civilization.

This is where I belong.

The jaguar circles me, and I hold my breath, closing my eyes, thinking this is it. But as the cat circles, it rubs against me, again like a house cat. Like it knows me. Again, I laugh at the absurdity of it.

In the distance, I hear something.

A muffled scream. A wet, blood-curdling scream.

I try to push it out of my mind, concentrating on the

sensation of the pink cat's fur against my skin. These final moments on earth are mine to savor.

The screaming crystallizes, becoming sharp and loud and unavoidably close.

My eyes shoot open.

I look up the path, and I see the cat's tail flying wildly back and forth as it struggles with something on the ground. Another scream erupts.

Collin.

The cat is attacking him.

I scramble to my feet, unsure what to do.

I stand there, shocked into freezing.

Neon red blood sprays across the air, spinning outward like confetti. The cat is agile, twisting and turning itself until its jaws clamp down on Collin's throat and in an instant, there's a crunch and he goes silent.

The only sound that can be heard is the cat's heavy breathing with a human's neck in its mouth.

I stand there, staring at the cat.

And like it can feel my gaze, it lets go of Collin and turns its attention to me.

It's so beautiful.

Pink, purple, and teal. The cat glows.

I can't look away.

And then I feel woozy, dizzy. Falling to the ground, I hit my head.

All the lights go out.

THIRTY-SEVEN

I'M FALLING through space until I hit the ground, hard.

I gasp for air and shoot straight up.

Breathing heavily, I realize I'm lying on the jungle floor. I spin, looking everywhere for the cat. And at the same moment I realize it's not here, I realize that, even though the cat is gone, I'm not alone.

My eyes land on him.

Lying next to me, unmoving, is Collin.

And his neck is a shredded mess. I look away. But after a moment, curiosity gets the best of me, and I want to see what happened.

His jugular is torn wide open, his skin flayed.

The kind of injury you only see when an animal attacks.

I stare at the inside of his throat, looking at it with a clarity that I haven't had all night. It's then that I realize dawn is barely beginning to break.

The night is over.

I look at Collin again, searching for the cat's tracks, but I don't see them. And it's then that I realize I'm clutching something in my right hand like my life depends on it. My knuckles ache to release it.

I look down at it and see a sharp stick in my hand.

The end of it is coated in darkness.

Coagulated blood.

I drop it, scrambling backwards.

My breathing grows ragged, shallow.

I look around the clearing, and I can hear voices coming close. They're almost here.

My eyes return to Collin. A pair of flies buzz around his open throat. One of them lands on the red flesh that should be tucked neatly into his body. Just as quickly, it buzzes off.

I'm still staring at the flies when two men come traipsing through the rainforest. Immediately, I recognize one of them as Juan Miguel. The other looks like a police officer.

I kick the sharp little stick away, shoving dirt over it with my bare foot.

"Oh, God," Juan Miguel says as he takes in the scene.

The police officer looks at Collin but turns his attention to me almost immediately.

"Are you okay?" He asks with a heavy accent. "Hospital?"

It's then that I realize I'm shaking.

I nod my head.

"I'm okay," I say. "I don't need the hospital." I shake my head.

He nods, understanding.

"We will get you out of here," he says.

Another officer enters the clearing and the two of them get me up.

"My husband," I say.

"We found him," the other officer says. "You come with us."

And I let them take me away.

THERE'S a police van and an ambulance at the visitor's center, and Juan Miguel gives me fresh clothes and a blanket when we arrive. I change, numb to my circumstances, and not really ready to process the fact that everyone has died.

I repeat it to myself, trying it out. How does it sound?

Surreal.

It can't be.

Every time I say it, I tuck it back, telling myself that I'll deal with it later.

And I don't allow myself to think of Steve.

As soon as his name comes to mind, I shove it down, replacing thoughts with darkness. Nothingness. I can't go there.

I have to get out of here. I just need to survive until I can deal with this.

I hear the police talking to Juan Miguel. I listen, my high school Spanish so rusty that I only pick out a few words, but one registers.

Murderer.

And when the officer says it, he glances back at me. Juan Miguel looks at me, too, suspicion seemingly on his mind. And I feel the first flutter of anxiety. The first notion that this isn't over.

They think I killed them.

The realization hits me, and I sit with it, like a big silent animal sitting near me. I feel its oppressive mass. And then a resolution comes to mind.

I won't live the rest of my life in a Peruvian prison.

I didn't kill them.

And I needed to defend myself against Collin.

But I can see it all play out.

The foreigner comes and thinks she can get away with murder. Maybe she wanted her husband's money. Maybe she went crazy. An ayahuasca trip gone wrong. I can see all the clever headlines it will prompt in both English and Spanish.

I shake my head as I imagine it.

No.

This isn't how it's going to end.

I look back over at the officers, and one of them is walking toward me.

"Mrs. Silkwood," he says. "Would you mind coming and answering some questions in town?"

"Not at all," I say.

There's not much else I can say. And it strikes me how vulnerable I am. I know nothing of Peruvian law. A laughable realization when I combine it with the fact that I was willing to risk everything without that knowledge.

Jesus Christ.

I'd been out of my mind.

And for what?

The thought of Steve returns to me and I'm struck by abject sorrow.

I force it down.

I have to answer questions right now. That's all that matters. I can do that.

"We will go now," the officer says. I offer him a polite smile and stand up. Juan Miguel comes over and I hand him the blanket, thanking him. He quickly tries to tell me how he went to town immediately when he realized we were missing and that he's sorry it worked out like it did.

The entire conversation is a blur.

I can't imagine anything that he could have said that would have made any good difference, so I just nod, and I thank him for getting help.

I'm a little unnerved by how close the officer walks to me as we go out to the police van. I glance back toward the hut and see two men carrying a body in a white sheet that's been stained red near the head.

I try to judge how tall the body is. Is it Steve?

The thought raises that horrible sorrow again.

And it occurs to me in that moment that this might be the last time I ever see him. That last night, as he lay dead on the rainforest floor, was the last time I would ever touch him.

A memory comes to me. Him laughing.

He had this laugh that could fill up a room. It was infectious. And when he got going, you would laugh, too, despite yourself. Even if you didn't think the thing that made him laugh in the first place was funny.

A numbness washes over me as I get into the van. The officer closes the door and soon another officer joins us. I assume that there is at least one staying here to investigate the scene.

The ride back is strange. Sunlight shines down on the town of Iquitos in a way that it seems it shouldn't after a night like last night. It makes me think of all the terrible nights the sun chose to continue to rise, unflinching and unmoved by whatever horrors passed between the hours of dusk and dawn.

That's the hardest thing about grief, isn't it?

That the world doesn't just stop.

It feels like it should, but as I look at the streets of Iquitos, it's teeming with life that will go on, unaffected by everything that happened last night. So many horrible things happen all the time and we're unaware of most of them.

It just so happens that this time, it's happened to us.

To Steve.

And it's my fault.

I steel my resolve as we pull up to the police station. At the visitor's center, I collected my cell phone, and they haven't confiscated it from me yet. A good sign, I think. If that happens, they're arresting me.

I try to calm myself down.

No one else survived. It's my word against the evidence.

And if I can make those two things line up, I'll be out of here.

I hate myself for being a coward.

Even now, as I'm planning my escape, I feel nothing but self-loathing.

Maybe I really always have been this cold, calculating person. God, how I wish I could have just lived out the rest of my life as the version of me that didn't remember how terrible she was.

At the station, one of the officers leads me into a small room that looks disturbingly like an interrogation room. I'm grateful when he doesn't shut the door.

He asks my name. Where I'm from. What I'm doing in Peru and how long we were staying. I tell him the most bland version of the backstory I can manage.

And then it comes down to it.

"What happened out there?" he asks.

I take a deep breath.

There's a part of me that wants to tell him it's so much more complicated than just what happened out there. That there's so much more to the story.

But I remind myself that I need to get out of here.

"I think it was the ayahuasca," I say. "I think it really affected Collin's mind in a horrible way. I don't know if he had been planning something like this or what, but he said some things about being in love with me and wanting to get everyone else out of the way."

The officer takes this down, not looking up at me for a moment. But when he does, it occurs to me that he's already made up his mind.

"What happened to Collin?" The officer asks.

"A jaguar attacked him," I say.

I try to come off as cool and collected as I can. I take a sip of the water he gave me right after he put me in here. The tiny Styrofoam cup shakes in my hand and he clocks it.

"Aftereffects of the ayahuasca," I say. My calm exterior crumbles a bit as his eyes linger on me.

"We will look for evidence of a cat," he says. "While we do, you stay in Iquitos."

I nod vigorously, like I want to get to the bottom of this as much as he does.

"Yes, of course. Anything to help."

He escorts me out and hails a cab for me. I tell him that I'll go to the hotel, and I won't leave.

But as soon as I'm in the taxi, I navigate to the banking app.

I see the Black Label Trading account. The money is still there.

I look up flights to Cuba. And one leaves from Lima tonight.

THIRTY-EIGHT

I PACK QUICKLY once I'm back in the room.

And then I book the flight to Cuba with a connecting flight to Lima. Late tonight, I'll land in Havana.

When I realize I've gotten everything together, I take a deep breath and call the taxi. My nerves are frayed and right on the edge as I arrive at the small airport. There's an hour before the flight from Iquitos to Lima.

I find a little magazine rack and buy several English magazines for the trip. I flip through them as I sit in the airport waiting for the signal to board my plane.

Finally, it comes, and I get onto a little puddle jumper with about ten other people.

As the plane gathers speed on the runway, my heart beats faster.

Before I know it, we land in Lima and I'm off to my connecting flight.

I shuffle through the aisle of the plane, politely excusing myself as I bump into people. It strikes me that I'm having to pretend everything about this is entirely normal. I wonder when I'll fall apart. And I hope that when I do, I'm never able to put myself back together.

Not after what I did to Steve.

I deserve every bit of pain and then some.

I'll carry that forever, and I hope, even in another life, he doesn't forgive me.

That will haunt me forever.

But when the plane takes off and I feel the sensation of it lifting into the air—the point of no return—I feel a rush of relief.

I close my eyes.

And when I do, I see him.

That laugh again. I can hear it.

And it's in that moment that I feel something happening within me.

A fragmentation.

Myself, shattering into a million little pieces that I could never put back together even if I wanted to. And it's exquisite. It's a release.

I see the jaguar.

The pink, purple, and teal jaguar with its glowing green eyes.

I stare into those eyes, and I meet myself for the first time.

The darkness and the light of my soul, mingling together in a cosmic stew, reflected back at me in that jaguar's eyes.

Just then, my phone rings, surprising me.

I get it out of my purse and look at the number. International.

Without thinking, I pick it up.

"Hello?"

"Mrs. Silkwood?"

"This is she."

"We have some additional questions for you. We will pick you up at the hotel," an officer says on the other end of the phone.

"That's fine," I say.

"I'm sure you want to settle this as much as we do," he says, a threat in his voice.

"You have no idea," I say in return. "See you soon."

I hang up, flag down a flight attendant, and order a Bloody Mary.

THE PLANE TOUCHES down in Havana late that night. I watch the city come into view as we fly over Cuba, circling and preparing for landing.

I'm one of the last to get off the plane, and as I do, my heart beats faster. I'm waiting for someone to stop me. To say that I have to fly back to Lima, and then back to Iquitos. I'm waiting for someone to call me a murderer.

But no one does.

The flight attendant simply smiles at me as I get off and thanks me for flying American.

I grab my luggage at the carousel, and I pause at the sliding glass doors that lead out of the airport. People flood into the baggage claim area and flood out into the pickup area in equal numbers. I watch them all come and go and I stare at the double glass doors in front of me. They open and close, open and close.

And I realize that it's happening.

I've made it.

I survived.

Digging into my purse, I pull something out. The green *Jaguar* keychain.

The trip of a lifetime.

I rub it between my fingers.

I take a deep breath, join the crowd, and walk out into the night air of Havana.

ACKNOWLEDGMENTS

First, I want to thank my mom for her endless support when it comes to making it possible for me to write. She believed from the very beginning when we told people we were going to New York City for me to pitch my first thriller in 2017. Everyone thought we'd lost our minds, and I started to think they might be right. Thank you, Mama Vinge, for your unwavering faith in me and my dream.

Thanks to my family for always being there for the highs and lows of this insane career. What a dream it's been, and I'm so grateful for each of you.

Thank you to Katie and Johnetta, who are my core colleagues. The two of you keep me sane when I'm about to go around the bend.

Thank you to Ann, my personal assistant. Finding you was exactly the right next step at a time when I really needed it. You make everything so much easier and even more fun! You're a rockstar and I'm so thankful to you for all that you do, and all that you did to make this launch a success!

And most of all, thank you to each and every reader for taking a chance on my stories. I hope they've entertained you, kept you up all night, made you gasp, and ultimately provided some entertainment in a world that can sometimes be difficult to face. You all keep me going and I love hearing from each and every one of you! Keep those messages coming!

This book is particularly close to my heart. It was actually the first idea I had for a true psychological thriller, even before *The Getaway* and *Swingers*.

My family often asks me where I get my ideas, and the answer is probably unsatisfying and far less glamorous than readers might hope it is.

They come from anywhere and everywhere. The most mundane thing to anyone else might inspire a murder plot in my mind.

This one kind of sprung from a few wells: a moment on a trip to Norway to see my family in 2016, an episode of a Josh Gates show, and the movie *Anaconda*. If you haven't watched it, you're missing out. It's right up there with *Lake Placid*. And if you know me at all, you know *Lake Placid* is a valid religion in my eyes.

On the trip to Norway, we stopped at a particularly big waterfall and my cousin told me a story about a German couple that had visited. The husband kept telling the wife to back up until she backed up right off the cliff and fell to her death. Turned out, it was intentional.

My subconscious tucked that story away for another time, like it often does. Earlier this year, I found out that luxury cruises down the Amazon River are a thing you can do. I also watched Josh Gates's special about the afterlife. In one episode, he chronicles his ayahuasca experience in South America, which he finds to be profound and terrifying, all at once.

As someone with a spicy neurodivergent brain to begin with, the idea of tripping balls in the jungle sounded like my idea of a horror story. But I was fascinated.

One day, randomly, these three things ran into each other in my brain and the vision of a woman being pushed from a luxury riverboat on the Amazon came to me. Shortly after that, the twist arrived.

I wanted to do this story justice, and I hope I did.

I hope you enjoyed it, and you'll consider following my journey as an author by checking out some of my other books, including one coming in February of 2024 that I think you might love.

Stay spooky.

ABOUT THE AUTHOR

I started writing when I was 7. The book was called *It Came Floating Up*. It was inspired by many trips to the beach and watching a few too many episodes of *The X-Files* with my grandmother. The book was about a monster lurking in the sargasso seaweed just off the coast of Corpus Christi. In the dedication, I wrote:

To my family, who has been there through everything.

I was 7. If only I'd known then what exactly *everything* would entail.

Since then, I've only gotten more dramatic and more obsessed with *The X-Files* and storytelling.

My books all have one thing in common: they are inspired by some element of truth either in my own life or something I pick out of a headline or a history book. Mostly, though, my writing is inspired by my own experiences and emotions, just blown up on a grander scale with a murder or two to make it exciting.

Just call me the Taylor Swift of psychological thrillers.

JOIN MY NEWSLETTER

Sign up now and get a free horror novella, The Body Snatchers. You'll also get updates, freebies, news about me and my dogs, plus book discounts and sales!

Sign up here:

https://BookHip.com/PZGBMZT

ALSO BY MARNIE VINGE

SHOP NOW

www.marniewritesthrillers.com

Psychological Thrillers

The Getaway

Swingers

For Rosie

I Remember Everything

Cold Blood

Women's Thrillers

The Way It Ends

What We Did That Night

Manspreader

The Blair Graves Files

The Haunting of Solomon House

The Holloway Hoax

The Vampire's Game

One Night in September

Short Horror Collections

Thicker Than Water

In Sheep's Clothing

The Reunion

Romance

Gunshy